LOZEN

LOZEN

BOB WRIGHT

LOZEN

This book is written to provide information and motivation to readers. Its purpose is not to render any type of psychological, legal, or professional advice of any kind. The content is the sole opinion and expression of the author, and not necessarily that of the publisher.

Printed in the United States of America.

ISBN   978-1-951913-11-3   (Paperback)
ISBN   978-1-951913-12-0   (Digital)

Lettra Press books may be ordered through booksellers or by contacting:

Lettra Press LLC
30 N Gould St. Suite 4753
Sheridan, WY 82801, USA
1 303-586-1431 | info@lettrapress.com
www.lettrapress.com

Lozen

 don't know where or when I was born. It was during the time of war with the NezPierce and the white man. That's all I know of this. My mother "Lozen" told me of her taking me from a wagon train that they were trying to turn back to the East. She told me of the blood that was spilled by both sides of the battle. She said she was fighting for her life. She told of how she took some of the white men to the Great Spirit in the battle. She was looking at me, as she told of this. She said the Great Spirit talked to her as she was fighting; and when she looked to my eyes, He said--- "ENOUGH" --- She then told me of taking me from the wagon as the warriors were burning them, and of how she sat on her horse holding me as we watched the wagons burn. I was very young at this time and have no memory of this.

She talked of being "Shun" from her tribe for taking me with her, and of riding to the forest to live without them. I remember a few visitors that came to our camp for my Mothers advice, but they were few. As I got older and started to understand the language, I realized, they were talking of me. They demanded I be returned to the whites. I remember her telling me this, as I looked into her steel Gray eyes. I noticed after talking to the others that her eyes were "different" She told me the tale of the wolf this night. She spoke of growing up with the eyes of a wolf. She told of fighting with the young in the tribe over this. She then told me of being named "Lozen" She spoke of being trained as a warrior. She said her father wanted her to learn to protect herself from the others. She told me her Father was from the tribe of the Apache, and it was "He" who named her. She took me to the river; she had me look at my eyes. She said they were as blue as the sky above. As I was looking, I asked why we were "Different"? She laughed at this. She held me and told me of the "Spirit" that gave us our eyes. She shook her head. She took out her flute and played the song of the Wolf. She wasn't finished but stopped. She then told me of meeting with the War Chief Joseph. She told me of a dream that he had. She told me of him seeing "two Lozen's". She said they were fighting with the "Bear and the Coyote". She then returned to her flute. When she was finished she looked at me smiling. I asked if it were "me" that the War Chief had seen?? She said I don't know this. She said he looked into the Lozen's eyes; He said the eyes were like they were on fire. Then returned to her flute. She stopped again; She said he told her to be ready for this battle; that it was sure to come; ----"like the thunder that rolls over the mountain"!!!----She picked up her flute and played the Bear and the Coyote. When she was done I asked her when this would happen? She smiled and said I don't know. She talked of seeing my spirit as she took me from the wagon. She told me my spirit was like the thunder and lightning. That it will consume your enemies! Entirely!!! She looked at me and laughed. I was scared now and held her tight. She told me don't worry!! The Spirit will tell her and I when the time is here. She said I would know it when my Spirit makes the;

"Thunder and the lightning roll over the mountains"

She never spoke much, but she would play her flute like she was talking with it. She used it to raise me with the tunes and tones that she played; it kept me centered on life. From the time I learned how to walk I was near her, never more then a step behind. She was a hunter that used the wind and the river. She listens to them, and let them guide her way through the forest. I still recall the second winter we were together, when she placed me in a tree. I watched as she left me to do battle with the bear. She used a long lance and she drew the bear from the cave. The Bear charged straight at her, and she stood like a pine tree. She jumped and twisted and impaled the bear behind his shoulder. The bear lay there bleeding and growled with his final breath. When her battle was done she cut the meat from the bear to dry in the sun. We lived in the home of the bear for two winters. She named me "XA'XATS" After telling me the legend of the Bear and Coyote, as we hung the meat to dry. The story was long with many words to keep. She would stop and play her flute between each episode. She kept me wrapped in the hide of the bear for the warmth of my body. She gave a chant to thank him for this. I remember the smell of the cedar bows she burned in the fire. The smoke would briefly fill the cave, and leave the scent of the cedar in the air. We had firewood stacked at the back of the cave. She took a branch from the stack and fashioned me a flute like hers. She would make a sound and stop and look at me till I copied the sound exactly. By the time spring came to the valley I was able to copy her flute. This was the first years of my life, I was around four or five now and she fashioned me a back pack and we packed up and left the Bears cave and went to the valley where the hunting was much better. We moved slowly as we left there, and she taught me to walk softly. We would take a few steps and listen to the wind. She taught me to make the sounds of the animals of the forest, as we walked with no talking. It made no difference to her if we found no game for the day. She would play her flute at night as we sat by a small fire. She would encourage me to follow her tunes.

It was about our fifth year together when we were following the tracks of a deer. We came across a tribe of a sub chief that my Lozen knew. They had done battle with the white army and they were suffering from wounds that they got from the battle. I helped Mother Lozen tend to their wounds. They just looked at me strangely. Mother Lozen told them I was in her "keep" I was giving them water and when I came to one of them he reached for my hair. He was just feeling it I guess. I had water in the skin and helped him to drink it. When I laid his head back to the ground he just kept staring at me. With his last breath he said "A-HO"- (which is look out) and passed his spirit to the Great one. I quietly told my Lozen of this. Her steel gray eyes were looking at me. She told me to move quietly to the forest. It was near dark out now and I hid behind a tree where I could watch. She kept tending the warriors, and after a time I heard horses running our way. The sub chief and the two men with him rode to Lozen and stopped. I could hear the turmoil in the Chiefs voice showing his anger.

Before he could lift his rifle Lozen slashed him with her lance. She then made him through the gun to the ground. With her lance at his throat she shouted to the other two they did the same. She then had them throw down their bullets too. She then told them to go!! The chief was shouting hate to her as he held his arm and turned and rode away. She told me they were demanding she give me to them. She finished bandaging the last one; She picked up a rifel and bullets. She said it had started now, and we moved on. I asked her of the horses?? She told me we don't need them, that they make too much noise. She told me of the tribes that were at peace with the whites. She told me of their sub Chiefs that refused to fight. She said when I am ready we will find them. I asked her if we were at war with them. She said; "Were not," but they "Are." She said for as long as we are together. We will be at War with both the Red and the White. I started crying and held her close to me. I told her it's not fair. She laughed and said no it isn't; that she had asked the great spirit the same thing when she took me from the wagon. She held me tight. When I quit crying, she told me we must keep moving. She told me that if we stop for more then a day that we risk being found.

The bow and arrows was the next thing she taught me. She had me stretch the string to the bow. I remember it took all of my strength to do this. She made stand still with an arrow ready to let go of it. She would make hold it as long as I could. The mussel in my arm grew stronger. I did this before she taught me of the aim. She started to train me to throw the knife now. She taught me of using my wrist. My body felt different now. My mussel was starting to grow. I would race her to the river at a dead run. By the end of the day I was tired. But she made me copy her songs. The next day we started to split our time between the aim; and throwing the knife. She made me lift a rock up down to build up my wrist. She then taught me how to throw with my wrist. And then there was the lance! She never let a day go by that I didn't practice with my lance. We would run next to each other and lift ourselves to the air with them and turn to strike. She called this the jump twist and turn. I was pooped!!!

We were hungry this night when stopped for dinner. We were down to the last of our food; Mother suggested we split up tomorrow to hunt for the antelope. I went to the south and mother went to the north. This is where she encountered the tribe of the NezPierce. They were many and took her captive. Three days had gone by waiting for mother. Two men rode into our camp. They told me of mother being held by the tribe. I wanted to take the life of the warriors. But I knew they would kill mother if I did this. They tied my hands and took me to their camp. They were going to trade me for guns. Mother and I were tied to a tree. They fed us but belittled Mother. She said nothing for the next two days. The Chief came to Mother to talk. She spit in his face and called him a coward. This made his anger grow. He struck her across her face and she demanded that she fight his "Champion" With his anger he brought him forward. He was a mass of mussel and growled like a bear. She spit at him too; and he struck her face. She then spit her blood in his face again. He demanded she be untied.

She was unarmed and stayed away from him when the fight started. He slashed her arm with his knife. She kicked his hand and the knife fell to the ground. She jumped and turned her body and kicked him again. She picked up his knife and spun in a circle and stabbed him. She then drove it deep into his mighty chest. It became quiet now. We were set free after this. She wished shame on the chief of the tribe. We returned to our camp and I took care of her wounds. I sewed up her arm as she played her flute. I was crying and asked her if she will be all right?? She asked that I speak of this no more. We spent two weeks there till mother stated to heal. We broke camp and started to walk. They followed us for three days till we were out of their territory. The chief shouted that we were never to return. Mother spit to earth and cursed the ground that they stood on. The Chief then stabbed mothers lance into the earth, and rode away. I picked up her lance and asked what we will do now?? We were traveling to the west and now we were moving south. She told me we must follow the water. She looked across the hills and pointed to a mountain. It looked so far away. Mother rationed our food and water and we traveled at night. It took three weeks to get there. We were both exhausted; we drank the sweet water from the spring by the mountain. Mother told me we must wait here to avoid traveling further to the south. She told me the spring is the only source of water for miles around us. We set up camp and waited,

I saw a small group of Northern Apache riding into the water. I shook mother to wake her. She greeted the warriors and stood before the sub chief. They showed her honor as they spoke. They talked of riding to the north after a battle with the whites. They were different then the NezPierce, much friendlier to my Lozen. She told me of being born to this nation. She was traded to the NezPierce. That was all she ever said of this. We camped with them for seven suns. They shared their food with us. They treated us like "Family" She told the tribe to move to the North East to the land where she did battle with the bear. They asked that we come with them. I was excited to hear this; these were a people that showed us their Love!!! Mother Lozen told them she couldn't. She had promised the Great One that she would journey to the Bitter Root Mountains. They left us a horse and a rifel. I started crying as I watched them ride toward the rising sun.

We were meeting people scattered across the country now. Mostly their tribes abandon them. They were in groups of the young and the old. Some asked for my help. Most ignored me. A few were ready to fight me. Mother kept them calm. She asked me not to fight with them. She said they are a defeated nation. We traded antelope that we hunted for another horse. She would talk to them quickly and leave them. I was learning of discrimination now!!! We traveled wide around the nation that mother was ban from. We just kept traveling north.

When we were traveling the prairie we were far away from everybody. She taught me to use the rifle. She spent much time on this till she saw me hit the targets with each shot. She then had me dig a hole and bury it. She told me of fighting the whites, and of how it attracts others when we use the rifel. She preferd her lance. She told me only use the rifle when I have no choice. After traveling many miles we came to an area of hills. They stood to the sky with no reason for this. There were many hills in our view. Mother Lozen took me to the top of one of them and told me to stay there. She talked of an attack on the white army that the people we met had told her of. She talked of her tribe moving to the north with the women and children to avoid being slaughtered. She told me of Eagle of the Sky who was leading the battle to slow down the army for the tribes escape. She talked of her respect for him, and of how he needs her help. When we arrived she talked with the chief. She told him she wished to fight no more, she was asked to tend the horses. She sent me to the next hill to watch the battle. I watched as the chief had his men posted on the hills on both sides of the trail. There were only about ten of them, but they were well armed with repeating rifles.

I had a much better view of the soldiers riding in then anybody else had. They looked endless riding in columns of four. The tribe was tucked into the narrows and waiting for the soldiers to ride on through. As I was watching I saw the army send a company of men to the side of them to ride around their flank. I was too far away from Mother Lozen to warn her of this. I had to make my mind up to go to war with the white men. I was looking at Mother Lozen far away, as she stood alone. I started crying and went down the backside of the hill. I wished to be with my mother.

There were at least twelve soldiers riding my way. They were splitting into four groups. I was half way to my mother when I came across the first of them, and a shot from the rifel was fired at me. I took cover behind the rocks and listen for the horses. I heard the hoofs of one riding my way. I looked at the lance my mother made for me. It looked like I would be using it. I gripped it tight in my hands. I jumped into his path and I used my lance to bring the soldier down. I was sick. I picked up his rifel and shot the second one. I took my lance to the top of the rocks and waited for the third to ride to me. With a scream I swung my lance; I took his life too. I picked up his rifel and the last one rode away. I kept moving to my mother. By the time I reached her she was in combat with the soldiers. I used one shot and dropped the one holding his guns aim to her. I ran and stood back to back with my mother now with my lance, as we were too tight to use firearms. With our lances we finished the battle with the other group of soldiers. We were both wounded but still standing. As I looked at the dead soldiers I felt the fury in my sole for the attack on my Mother. She calmed me; we went to the edge of the hill. Mother Lozen watched as the last of her tribe fell to the bullets of the soldiers. I quickly tied a tourniquet to mother's leg and grabbed two of the horses. We rode until nightfall; and stopped to tend to our wounds.

Mother had lost so much blood that she was weak from this. I settled her down near a creek and sewed up her leg. I kept a damp towel on it that I had torn from my clothing. With her head in my lap I prayed to the Great One to save her. The bullet had torn through her leg and it was now up to him. I kept her cool by the creek and waited for three days before she talked to me. She asked me to leave her there by herself. I shouted in her face and told her don't you dare leave me now!!! I told her I love you my mother!! And I need your guidance to travel the land. I watched as the pain was growing and kept her cool. I had one wound to myself where a bullet had grazed my leg. I washed it and kept it wrapped to stop the bleeding. I learned to ignore it, and kept tending my mother.

I heard a few horses coming our way. I covered Mother with branches from the trees. I saw three men riding following the tracks left from our horses. I took the horses up the creek and left them to graze. I took mothers quiver of arrows, and her bow with me and stationed myself where I had cover. Mother had taught me of this, that the time it takes to reload the rifel was the key. There were three of them. One was an Indian scout that was following our tracks. The scout was dismounted, and when I let go of my first arrow; it went into his leg and he was down. The two soldiers were riding to me and they fired their rifles hitting the tree near me. I stood with an aim on the soldier and my arrow stuck deep in his chest, and the last soldier reloaded and took a shot at me. The second he fired I had my bow ready, and took him to the ground too. Both soldiers lay dead, but their scout was sitting there. I picked up my lance and went to him. I squatted down about five feet away. I looked to his eyes, I could see he was NezPierce, and I asked him why he leads the white men to us? He looked to my eyes and said he had heard of me, that he didn't believe it was true!!! I stuck my lance to his throat and asked him again!! He said our tribe was conquered and of how they find women and children abandon along the trail, that he does this to save what he can. As I looked in his eyes I saw truth in his talk. I had him sit still and took his knife from his scabbard and asked him again to sit still. I pushed my arrow through his leg and cut the point from it. When he recovered from this I pulled the shaft from his leg. I wrapped his leg with a bandage and tied it up with a belt from the soldier. I was sitting in front of him now looking to his eyes. I told him to rest a few days before he rides. He asked of the "Other" I told him, she is my "Mother" whom you and the soldiers have wounded. That I let you live that you may tell them of us, to leave us alone. That we wish to travel our path; with no wish to kill you; I told him that if we are attacked again, that we will rise up with fury. I then looked to the soldiers who lay dead. I told him this brings sadness to my heart. I looked back at him and told him if I have to do this again, that I will do this with no heart for the white or the red. I said again; just leave us alone. I then covered the soldier's faces and returned to my Mother. I had the warrior at a distance away where I could see him. He asked to talk with my Mother. I went to him and told him to remain silent. I told him of my talk with her. That she told me to take your life from you so we wouldn't be followed. He looked at me with fear in his eyes. I told him I wont kill you, that I need him to spread the message. Too just leave us alone.

After the third day of holding her, I placed her head on a blanket of tinder. I took one of the horses with me to the other side of the hill. I said a prayer to the Great one, and slaughtered the horse; and brought the meat back to camp to cook it. I fed mother the best I could, and I watched as her strength grew. I took a portion to the warrior and checked on his wound. He asked to feel my hair. As he did this he told me it's as soft as it looks to be. I said nothing to him and went to my Mother. I was ready to move now, and I went to the warrior, I told him he was ready to ride now, to go; and tell them; to just leave us alone. I helped him to his horse and he looked at me. He promised to do what I asked of him. I placed Mother on the last horse and I walked for days to the timber where I felt at home. I now hunted the game in the timber and brought it to our camp. I kept the fires small and the nights were cold. I barely had enough clothing to cover myself, and kept mother warm when night fell on us. I was used to the area that I hunted and took the rifel with me this time in case I needed it. I spotted a group of deer that was up the creek from me, and took my aim on the large buck. I drug him to camp and skinned him out and laid the stretched hide out to dry. I hung the meat in the sun and dried it too. Mother Lozen was now wanting to try walking. I steady her to my shoulder and she walked. It had been a month since the battle and we still hadn't talked. She asked why I saved the warriors life. I told her I wanted to send a message to the men who hunt us like we are deer; that I just want to be left alone. She said she fears that I have started a legend. That it will follow us no matter where we go. I told her, "I love you mother" that she is a legend in my eyes. She told me that she is a NezPierce warrior. She spoke of seeing a cloud forming on the horizon. She looked at me and told me of trying to hold the cloud back so it wouldn't move over us. She said she sees us in the clouds fighting with evil and of a battle with much blood being spilled. I finished checking her leg. I told her I only see the dust the buffalo raise. I told her of a dream that keeps coming to me, that I only see us watching the herd. She asked me the size of the herd? I told her it's larger every time I see it after a battle. She said this is good. We need more time.

I was heating the venison over the fire when she asked me to sit with her. She talked of the man called Eagle of the sky. She talked of the battles they were in together. She had asked him to wait for her, after taking me from the wagon train. I felt her sadness come over me. I asked her if she wished she hadn't done this?? She said NO!! That the Great Spirit came over her that day!! And told of doing what he tells her to do. She held me close and told me we were bonded together till he calls her name. I now felt her Love for me. I told her of my fear and hate in my heart as we battle with the soldiers. She told me she had seen this in her dreams. She said this was why I was raised up alone. She said with so much blood being shed that She was to show me both sides of the battle. She said she had hidden me from this for too long now, and that this is where it starts.

She taught me of the Lance, the knife, and of the bow and arrows. She taught me of fighting with the Red and the White. With the red She taught me to use my "Ferocity" and with the white she taught me of the calm. I understood now that which she taught me. She prayed that I would never use this knowledge again. When we were done with a lesson one night; I asked her why we love each other so much!! She spoke of our battles, that we laid our life out on a line for each other without a thought of anything else. She said when she felt my back touching hers; that she knew she had chosen with wisdom; to defend the bond that holds us. She asked me if I felt the Spirit walk with us as we travel the land??? I told her of the feeling in my heart when I took the lives of the white soldiers. I told her it was hard to do this, but the love of my mother was so great!!! I had no choice. I told her that I felt the spirit talk to me before I pulled the trigger. She picked up her flute and played it softly as I held her tight.

This went on this way for the next year as I grew. I grew mussel in my body and the length of my steps grew to easily match my mothers. She would hide from me and I would track her. I remember the one time I found her. I was sneaking up on her. I thought I had finally won the game. I ran to tackle her, and she pulled on a rope; and I was hanging upside down from a tree. This was the first time I saw her laughing. Her eyes were sparkling as she let me down. I hugged her and was laughing too. She played the song of the Antelope and I followed her lead. When we finished the song she was looking at me, and said I was ready to travel.

After many days of traveling; we came across a wagon train that was attacked by the tribes. We saw an Indian scout with them. There were white men and women tending the injured. Mother asked me to ride to them and ask if they wish for our help. The Indian scout was afraid for his life. He wished us a blessing if we would do this. I motioned to mother to ride on in. I couldn't do nothing but try to stop the blood. One of the men was a white doctor. He was shouting orders to everyone there. He came to me as I was applying pressure to a man's wounds: He took over as he smiled at me. Mother and I were busy this day and night. The whites accepted us. The cook from the train fed us. And we lay down to sleep. We were up first the next morning ready to ride. The scout and the doctor came to us to talk. The doctor thanked mother and I for our help. Mother asked him not to speak of this. She told him it would only bring the thunder of the tribes down on us. The doctor agreed with her. He gave her a long warming hug. We rode away.

We had more battles with the soldiers. We had no choice but to protect ourselves. We had battles with the tribes too! They wouldn't listen to my mother. We tried to stay out of their way. The war always found us. I had hardened my heart till I fought alongside my Mother with vengeance. I felt no regret in my soul. She now asked me of taking the life of the red man. I laughed. I told her I don't even think about it anymore. I told her I am ready to battle all that we meet now. Some are Good! And some are bad.

She continued my training to make me a warrior with using a spear to defend myself. She taught me to throw it and use it like my lance. She made me use the heavy spear to build the mussel in my arms. She called it a "one use" weapon. She said once you throw it that it's gone!! She taught me to use the lance that we carried, with twisting and turning. This was her weapon of choice!! With an end in her mind; she would hold it over me. Then smile and lift me to my feet. Mother taught me of using the ax for a weapon. She had me throw it with power that comes from my wrist. She tied a feather to a tree and I practice till I severed the feather. She then told me I need a longer lance. She said I had grown. We walked to the forest and she felt the trees. She would stop and shake them and give them a nod. She was shaking a tree as she was walking by it; she turned to me and said this is the "One" We dug the roots from the bottom of the tree, and let it dry in the shade. After a week of drying she started crafting it into a lance. We worked a week or more on the lance. She would stab it in the ground while we practiced other things. She would stop and check it with her hands as it dried in the hot sun. Sometimes wetting it down with brine. She added the knife to the back of the lance. She used a knife from the white army. She taught me to use both ends of the lance, to defend myself when I battled with the many!!! She crafted it into a thing of beauty. She carved a small bear head on the heel of the lance. She asked me to carry it with pride!! As I stood there with the lance by my side; She smiled and said I was ready for my next steps in her teaching me.

I will never forget using mother for target practice. She gave me a knife and an axe and told me to attack her. She just stood there unarmed and dared me!!! She then stared at me with her eyes of steel. With her body only she would avoid every attempt that I made to attack or throw them at her. She taught me to do this no fear of a man who does this to me. She said to think like the fast Fox. She taught me watch the man's hands, not to look to his eyes. She taught me never to engage a man when I have no weapon in my hand. She said if I was disarmed to keep at least ten feet away. She taught me to roll and jump to my feet; as I avoided the knife and the ax that was thrown. I think she spent the most time teaching me this. She kept it up till I was better then her. We rested one night when she said I was ready for the next step of my life. She pent the next several nights telling me tales. They all had a meaning to them. I used the tales as I lived my life. As we played our flutes; She told me the stories. Her doing this put strength in my life. This is where she told me the story of the Gold miner. She told me of the map on his knife, She told me of the way he would throw to the ground when he was threatened with an attack on him, and dare them to pick it up. She said he let their greed get the best of them first. She said he would laugh at them as they circled the knife. She said he would throw dirt in their face and grab the knife and take them down. She said he wasn't Big!! She said he was "smart". She said nobody ever saw the map on his knife!!!

My hair was long and blond as I grew. Mother Lozen kept it fashioned like hers. She kept the feathers of the Chickadees. She tied them to my hair and played a tune to the birds that gave them. She taught me to listen to the birds for their moment of silence. When this happens it's for a reason that they stopped. Sometimes it was a hawk that was watching them. And sometimes it was men moving. She taught me to live as a part of nature with her love of me. She taught me to protect our lives.

We were out on the prairie when we came across two dead warriors. We buried them under the rocks. We found their horses and mother decided to teach of war with horses. She taught me to hang to side to protect myself. She taught me to swing my lance from their back. She taught me to shoot my arrows from him. She taught to jump from his back at a full run. It was the end of summer when she was done. We had a battle with the white soldiers that sent us back to the forest. Mother was wounded in her leg. She had me remove the bullet. I did the best that I could. I wrapped it and life moved us along.

Mother was still having a pain in her leg where she was wounded. She told me she thought there might still be a piece of the bullet in there. We were near "Boise" now and I demanded she see the white doctor to get it "Fixed". She struggled with me over this!! And I demanded that she do this. We rode into town under the glare of the people there. They looked at mother and I with a look of –"Shock"—We asked an Indian guide from the wagon train where the doctor was at, He said he would ride with us. He mounted his horse and took us to the doctor's door. He had obviously heard of our legend. He helped me get mother in his office, and a crowd was gathering outside his door. The doctor said I had got her here just in time. He said she would never have lasted another day. Mother was "delirious" now and the doctor went to work. The crowd outside was getting noisy now. The scout and I went to the door. I asked him to interpret for me. He smiled and said it would be an honor to do this. We stepped out the door to look over the people. I shouted in "Sahaptian" that this is my mother. He told them in "English" The crowd was now quiet!! I said if any man or woman has a problem with this!!! That they face it with where I stand. He repeated it. One man answered me with a question??? He asked if we were the two who took the life of the soldiers?? After he told what I was asked; - I said "Yes" and the red Warriors too!!! He repeated it. The man then called me a savage!! He repeated it. I asked him if he held a gun to my mother!! What he would expect me to do?? He repeated it. I said make it your choice!! "That we did the right thing"; He repeated it. I told them I would take the life of the first one who threatens my Mother!!! He repeated it. I then looked deep in his eyes and asked him what he would do if it were his mother that was threatened?? He repeated it. They were quiet now. I asked them to leave!! He repeated it. The crowd was now walking away. They were mostly gone except for one white girl. She shouted out to me from the ground below us. My interpreter told me she was from the wagon train. That she asks for my help to find her mother. He said; the tribe of the NezPierce captured her. And that she loves her very much!!! I knew how she felt about this. I had him bring her to the Doctors office. She came in crying and knelt before me. I lifted her up, and looked in her eyes! I had him tell her to stop this now!! That crying will do you no good. I asked the scout where the wagons were going. He said to the other side of the "Blues" I told him of Coeur-d-Alene, that this is where we were headed too, that I would speak with my mother when the doctor is done. The scout said he would speak with the sheriff. He promised his honor for us when he was leaving. He said he would protect us any way he can. He asked that I watch over the white girl while he was gone. He smiled and called us Tonka and Lozen. I smiled back and asked him to run. I sat there and held the white girl. I took out my flute and played; ----"The Mother I Honor"---- With her head in my lap she lay sobbing. I saw the love of her mother. It made me feel this as I brushed her hair with my hand. I remembered almost loosing my mother while traveling the land. Half of my soul was on fire. The other half gave love to our mothers.

The doctor came out and started to smile. He held her head as I slipped out of the chair. He softly laid her head back to the couch. He showed me some fragments of bullet that he removed. He next took me to Mother. Using sign language he asked me to let her sleep. I gave her a kiss and said a prayer over her. The doctor took me to the door. I turned and whispered "N'De Varlebena" to mother. She awoke quickly and gave me her smile.

The scout returned with the wagon master. Seems they had been here for a week waiting to let the Indian problems to stop. He told me of a sub chief that held the girls mother for a ransom. They were afraid to meet with the chief. I asked them to wait till I spoke with my mother of this. I told them I know how the white girl feels; I asked him what the chief demanded for her return?? He said rifles and ammunition. I laughed, and said that's what I thought. I asked him to try to trade some of their livestock. The wagon master nodded his head to me and left us. I asked the guide for another day. I said that I would considerer his request if the wagon master fails. I said I had seen so much blood already spilled!! That it should make no difference to me now. I then asked him "Where does it stop" They quietly gave me a day. I sat there playing my flute. I was running this through my mind. I didn't want to furnish them with weapons; as I looked at the "white girl"; that lay on my lap. I was brushing her hair with my hand. The wagon master came in and sat beside me. He said he took two beef cattle to the chief and asked to trade them to him for the girl's mother. He said I don't know you!! But the chief knows of you. He said you killed his brother. He said to send the yellow haired Tonka to bring him the guns; he said he would take your life. He said this was the only way he will trade for the mother. He then said, this was all he said!! I had Buck thank him for trying. At least he bought us one more day. I Really needed Mother now. I felt that I had the ability to do this. The only thing missing was the blessing of Mother. I sat there thinking and playing my flute!!

The Doctor said I could talk to her now. The girl tried to follow me. I held my hand up to the girl. I went to the bedside of Mother. I said I wish I had better news. Her face turned sour. She asked what this was about. I told her of meeting the girl. I told her of the ransom. I told her of the Chiefs demands. I then told her of the Chiefs wish to kill me!! I asked if she knew of any way to stop this. I said I didn't want to be the cause of her Mothers death. I was more worried about her mother then fighting the Chief!! Mother said; give me my flute. I saw it on the table and handed it to her. She played it for fifteen minutes or more. She then asked to meet the white girl. I had the scout bring her in. Mother patted on her bed and she sat with her. Mother reached for her hand and she took it. She was crying as mother lay there reading her eyes. She turned to me suddenly and asked me if I felt the Bear?? or the Coyote?? I laughed and told her defiantly the "BEAR" She returned to her flute. She stopped and was looking at the girl; and told me she can't help me with this. She said she feels her love for her mother. Mother was staring off to the clouds!! She told me I would have to challenge their "Champion" to gain all their respect. She said the chief would be held to the side by his tribe. She said I would have to do it this way or fight all of them. She then asked how many there were in his war party?? I asked my interpreter to come in with me. He answered six to mother. She said that's what she thought. Mother asked him; how far away are they? He told her only a mile out of town!! She said this is "good" They are sure of themselves!! She next asked of the "BIG" one!!! The scout asked how she knew of this?? She laughed and told him she grew up with this knowledge. She asked me if I remember the twist and attack that she taught me?? I told her I nearly used it when we arrived. She said I would finally fight with the Bear!!! She chuckled to think of the bear when I use this move. She reminded me to lift myself with my lance, and kick him in the face. I said I know this Mother. She returned to her flute. She asked the scout to ask the girl if she wished to go with me. The girl said she would do anything to get her mother back!!! Mother then smiled at her. She had the scout tell her this will never happen, that she would be in the way of the "Spirit" She asked me if I remember the map on the knife handle. I said, "Yes" and we both chuckled!! She said challenge their champion. She sat there shaking her head. She said she "couldn't" be with me this time, my daughter. She asked that I follow her instructions to the end. She started to cry. She said to think of the lives that I would save. She next said to show her my face. I knelt over her on the bed. She slapped me so hard that I saw stars in my eyes!!! She gave me a small smile, and wished me well. The white girl was crying. She didn't understand this. I sent them both back to the wagons. Mother was worn out from this. She held her flute as she fell asleep.

I rode to the wagon train to talk with the wagon master. He asked me what happened to my face. I said @%%%$# my mother gave me permission to help you. The scout looked ready to cry. I asked for the best horse and a new knife. I said I would leave tomorrow. The scout asked me how many men would I need?? I told him "none", that they would just get in my way. He asked me if I were "Sure" I held my cheek and nodded yes to him. I asked him where I could sleep. I stayed in the white girls wagon this night. The scout delivered the new knife to me. I tied leather around the handle of the knife. Her name was Melanie Roberts. She promised to stand guard over me this night. And I fell to her bed like a "Rock".@$^$%%$#.

I was up early the next morning. Melanie fed me breakfast. I adjusted my jaw to where I could chew. @#$$$#@ I had the scout bring me both of the horses. He put the knife in the scabbard. I told him if I'm not back by midnight tonight!! Don't bother to come looking. The whole wagon train watched me ride away. They stood quietly in disbelief. I raised my lance to the air and screamed out for revenge on the war parties tribe. I had both horses running as fast as they could.

I saw their campfire burning. I was a mile away from them now. I tugged on the knife to make sure it was ready, I added the knife that mother fashioned to the butt of my lance; and rode into their camp. The sub chief came to my horse. I told him I buried the guns on the hill. He said he feels a legend in front him. I asked him to see the white woman. He shouted to the braves and they brought her out of the tent.

I asked him to see his "Champion" next. He stood there looking at me. I held my lance to his throat!! He hollered and a brave with a chest the size of a bear, came walking to stand with the chief. I drew the knife from the sheath and landed it at there feet. Holding my lance to the chief I told them there's a map on the handle that leads to the guns. I jumped from my horse and dared him to pick it up. He drew his knife and slapped his chief out of his way. We were circling the knife with our eyes locked together. When he grabbed for the knife I sliced his arm. He fell and kicked me and I rolled to my feet, I opened a wound on his face. He was mad as a bear when he came at me again. I threw dirt in his face and opened another wound to his other arm. I finally got him "MAD" He slashed at my legs and I felt the blood running. I backed up to the knife and he slashed my shoulder. I twisted and stuck his legs and drew blood. I now had him limping; I dove for the knife, at the same time as he did. I was quicker then him. I lifted the knife to his belly. I stabbed him. As I looked to his eyes I drove it in further. He now lay there—"dead." It took both hands to remove it.

The sub chief asked if I had really brought them the guns. I put the knife back in the scabbard and I told him only the Great Spirit knows. He motioned to his men and they brought the woman to me. She tried to tell me I was bleeding. I helped her onto her horse. I told the sub chief that I would have stood beside him to fight. I told him he brings shame on his tribe when he captures the white women. I marked his arm with my blood. I asked him to ride in shame; that a true warrior would hope for a mountain to fall on him.

We turned to the horses and rode back to the wagon train. When we were near I slapped her horse on his haunches. I saw Melanie run to greet her. I had lost so much of my blood that I rode to the doctor. I woke up three days later. Mother was over me when I awoke. She said I gave them a scare!!! I asked her how long she's been walking??? She showed me her, !!$@#$#$$# splint. I had to laugh, but it hurt to do this. I looked at Mother and said the man was "Huge" I asked how she knew I would win the battle?? She smiled and told me she sent the Great Spirit with me. She told me she saw it in her dreams. I said MOTHER!! Your dreams are going to kill me!!! We both had to laugh. She said she just knew I could do it. She turned to me and smiled, and said that's what she trained me to do!!! I lay there thinking.---- "I don't know how I did this"!!!!----

A day had passed and they woke me up to eat. After this they told me of "Guests" I thought what in the world is a "Guest"??? The interpreters name was "Buck" He asked if I would meet with Melanie and her Mother. I said I would if my Mother stays with me. Mother nodded to him and he brought them in. Melanie ran in and held me as tight as she could. Her Mother held my hand. My mother just took on a view of this. But I thought I saw her smile!!! The doctor come in and asked how I was doing??? I had Buck tell him I felt like I was run over by a herd of buffalo!!! He laughed and checked the wound on my leg. He said between my mother and I; we were built out of steel. He laughed and said most men would just give up and die!!! After buck told Mother what he said; Mother told him that I am a legend. She smiled at me. She then asked him if he's ever seen a legend "DIE" He started laughing uncontrollably, the white girls didn't know what to do!!! I asked him when the wagons were leaving. He said tomorrow before they get stuck in the snow. Melanie was begging us to come with them. She said it was just she and her mother since the raid; that her father died in the battle. I had Buck tell her that her love is true. But she knows not what she asks us to do. I told her half of them love us!! But half of them "hate" us!!! I said she has her hands full just helping her mother. I said goodbye to Melanie and her mother. I gave them each a feather from my hair. The next morning Melanie brought me an apple pie. She squeezed my hand and ran. Mother said we must plan on leaving. She said our legend has caught up to us with its good and its bad. She said we are now the hero's of the white man. Till were attacked by the soldiers!! She said win, loose, or draw!! We are a "target" for all of them. I admitted it. I said I know what you mean. The doctor was good to us. He kept all out of our way. Two weeks later we slipped out of town in the middle of the night. We rode the horses for three days.

Mother turned the horses loose!!! and screamed at them till they ran. She stood smiling as she watched them. She told them to run with the wind. We walked slowly for seven days to the forest. Packing our gear the whole way. I never asked my mother! But the horses would have saved my soar feet!!! Those were the days!!!

I was sitting there watching a squirrel and playing my flute one morning. When it stopped and looked; I heard the crackle of the brush behind me. I saw the squirrel look across me and he started to chatter. I drew my lance to my lap and finished the song and just sat there and waited. I felt the spirit of an enemy approaching. I was waiting for the moment to come, and I held tight to where I was sitting. When I heard the steps close, I arose to defend myself with my lance. With my lance at his throat he dropped his ax to the ground and stood there ready to die. Mother Lozen appeared from nowhere and walked to me and looked to the eyes of the warrior. She said he was "Crow"

She then sat and took her flute and played a soft song of the birds. The soft music was like a signal. I lowered my lance and the warrior reached for his ax. I stabbed his hand with my lance and looked at him. He tucked his hand under his arm and looked to my mother. She lifted her flute and continued her song as the warrior walked away. I picked up his ax and threw it to a pine tree near him and it lodged in the tree with a thud. Mother again stopped playing her flute as she looked at the warrior. With a wave of her hand she had the warrior take his ax with him and finished her song with a loooong last note. I knelt before her and looked to her eyes. She placed her hands on me and said a prayer. We then got up and kept moving to the west without a word ever being said of this. Her teaching went on and on.

It was summer and mother and I would wrestle each other. She taught me the grace of this with moves that use my weight to take her to the ground. She always won when this started, but I was starting to have victories over her. When this would happen we would play the song of victory on our flutes. We had moved far from the valley of the bear now and mother Lozen and I built our winter lodging. We were near "Baker city in Oregon. The town was full of miners and Orientals. Mother was busy explaining this to me!! They had a "Color" that was different. When they spoke it was different. Nothing mother told of this made any sense. We were working on our winter clothing when Mother heard something!!! We ran to the edge of the hill and watched the engineers and Orientals walking the path for the railroad. We had seen the people driving stakes in the ground for the last month. There were crews of men working the forest for the "Ties" that they place for the rail. She saw one man that she thought was "Apache" I asked her if we should talk to him?? After a long silence she said she wanted me to go talk to him and see what there doing. I looked at her and said "Thanks" She just smiled.

The yellow people were so busy pointing at me and jabbering at each other that it scared me. I ran to the Apache man. Turns out he was "Navaho" our language was similar but different. I spotted mother looking over the hill. I gave up and pointed to her. The man just started waving at her to come down!!! He spoke to the other men and joined with mother and I. Mother came to me and asked what they were doing?? I started laughing. I said Uhhhhh!! They're putting in the railroad!!! She said "oh" The man's name was "Atsa" (which is Eagle) that we talked to. He shown mother honor when we met him; And best of all!!! He knew nothing of the %*&^$%@#^ Legends!!! We told him of our plans to winter here. He said they would stay till the weather shuts them down. He invited us for dinner this night; they had a "Chuck" wagon set up with an old man who was there to cook!! His name was "Honyauk" Nobody knew where that came from. He was white I think. I couldn't see his face thru his beard!!! Atsa introduced to us to him; and he scared mother so much that she ran from him. He was kind of loud. He called me a "pretty little girl" Atsa just said not to listen to him; He always talks tuff!! Honyauk took a handkerchief from his pocket and wiped off the lumber and had me sit to watch him cook. He was singing a song as he worked over the fire. I took the flute from my back and copied the sounds. He started dancing to the music as he cooked and just had more fun listening to me play then you can Imagine!!! Atsa told me he was "coo coo" I had to agree!!! I finally coaxed mother back to me. I made her play her flute too. They worked till it was dark and Honyauk rang a bell for dinner and it scared mother half to death. I hung onto her and refused to let her leave!! Mother didn't have fun this night. So I had it for her!!! I will never forget the look on her face when she tasted his dinner!!! That man could "COOK" I thought my belly would bust. It was the first time I had ever eaten "Beef"' I told mother we must learn from the Honyauk how to cook like he does!! With her mouth full she shook her head up and down!!! I had Atsa talk to him for me. He said "WHY HELL YES" Ill teach her to cook. He said as long as we help him with the dishes!!! Mother agreed!! That was too easy.

He taught me of bacon and sage and salt and pepper. He taught me of slow roasting and frying pan vittles and just gave me so much to remember. It lasted three weeks till the weather changed. They shut down for the snow. Atsa and Honyauk moved the wagon to the city I guess that's what it was!!! Baker was packed for the winter. I asked mother what we would have for dinner this night? She threw me a piece of sun-dried venison. I wanted to cry. But Honyauk's cooking was, Goooood while it lasted. We snuggled into our camp for the winter. I told mother it was the best three weeks of our life. She was thinking. She was playing her flute. She stopped and asked me what the men like "Best" She caught me off guard!! I sat there thinking. I picked up my flute. After about an hour I stopped and looked at Mother!! And said "Whiskey" She asked what I knew of making whiskey??? I told her of the still that Hanyauk used to make it. She asked is this hard to do??? I never paid attention to it. I told her I could ask him!!! She trusted me completely since I faced the "Giant" She asked me to find him in town. I told her the towns scare me!! She threw me a piece of venison!! I told her I'd do it first thing tomorrow!!!

I put the snow rings onto my moccasins. I told mother this might take a few days. She wrapped me in a blanket and I headed to town. Cursing my mouth the whole way. $%^%^^%^ I didn't know where to look for him!! I couldn't talk to anyone there. I found a spot by a tall building that was out of the wind and curled up to watch the street. I spent the night there by the building. I was so cold as I played my flute. My fingers were frozen. All I could think of was a fire!! One of the yellow people found me. He was chattering like a squirrel!!! I kept saying Honyauk and Atsa till he finally understood. They led me down the street carefully. My legs were asleep and I could barely walk. They took me to a large tent with a stove in it. I fell asleep just trying to get warm. The people were so nice to me. I had a touch of frostbite on my hands. They wouldn't let me go to look for the men. They fed me and kept me warm. After a day of; trying to talk to them. I figured out that they had moved on to the next town. The weather turned even colder now. With the wind they wouldn't let me go. I have to laugh. I found one yellow woman that lived there. I kept holding her and putting my head on hers. I started pointing to the camp of my mother!! And run back and give her a hug!!! They finally figured it out!!!! They hooked up a sleigh to a massive Belgian horse. Two of them came with me as I pointed the way. Mother was trying to clear the snow from the opening and failing at that!!! I started to load up what we had in the sleigh. She didn't argue either!!!

It must have been the worst winter ever. It either snowed or got colder each night. Mother and I worked on the hides, when our hands weren't frozen. We became friends with the people inside. Other then hand language we never learned how to talk to them. They kept us fed; but it was nothing like "Honyauk's cooking. Mother said we were lucky to have survived the winter.

It was early spring now. The snow was still high. The Chinamen were getting excited. We figured out that they were talking of a wagon train that was stranded for the winter. Seemed only three of them survived. They were white people that the town had rescued. We were thin but dang sure not like that!! Mother was watching them unload them from the sleigh. She started to cry and told me the story of this happening to some people from her tribe. They brought a young boy in on a stretcher. He was just skin and bones. I got excited when I noticed that one of the men helping them was "Atsa" I begged mother lets go see if we could help them. She wished the Spirit over me. I followed them into the building that they were taken to. I just started to cry. There was no one tending the boy. I checked to see if he was still alive!! His breathing was shallow. His arms were cold. His hands and feet were frost bitten. Mother had taught me of this. I asked Atsa for pans of water. I told him not to warm it to hot. I pulled up his pant leg and his legs were frost bitten too. I asked him of a tub large enough to fit him in it. He spoke to a man who had one. I just yelled to get it fast. I wanted to get him in before he gets warm. I remembered the pain when my hands were frost bitten. I asked Atsa to get mother. The yellow man understood what I was saying; and drug him out the door. I filled the tub with cold water. I next stripped off his clothing. They helped me get him in. I asked for a cup!! And they all just looked at me!! #$^%$## language anyway. One of the men who had rescued them was standing there with his coffee. I was pointing at his cup and he handed it to me and I filled it with hot water. I poured it around in a circle. I used my hand to mix it in. I felt his head and got another. Stirred it and felt his face. I did this four times when a lady took the cup from my hand. She started bringing the water. I slowed her down and kept touching his face. This is where mother came in. She was crying. I asked her to check his face. She checked his neck and said she felt his heart. I asked if I should add more of the hot water faster. She said no that I was doing fine. She kept her hands to his neck. She slowed it down now and kept track of his heart. I was stirring the water and mother said to add more hot water. She had me using two cups at a time now. We had been at it for more then an hour, when we saw him open his eyes. Mother said keep it coming slowly, she reached down a shut his eyes. It had been four hours since we started. Mother asked for some milk. She gave him a sip and set it down. She reached in and felt the water. She asked for a bucket full now. She had the lady helping us pour it in slowly. She gave the boy another sip. He reached up and touched her face. I felt her smile pass to the boy. He was in the tub for another two hours. She asked for blankets now and started to softly rub his skin. She asked the lady to help. She would feel his neck and give him a sip. She had us start dipping the water out. She folded a blanket and placed it over him where he was dry, and kept rubbing his body. The boy finally asked for his Mother. Atsa told us what he said. Mother said to tell him she's busy now; and smiled into his face. We finally got all the water from the tub, and mother had him wrapped up tight. She asked that we not move him. She would give him a sip. She left him in there for the night. He started complaining of pain. Mother said this is good. She said he will loose some toes and fingers but she seemed sure he would live. She had us warm the milk now. She kept giving him sips. She asked us to move him to the bed.

We moved him slowly and carefully to a bed now. Mother stayed with him. I don't know where she found the strength. He was starting to talk now. He was still asking for his Mother. He didn't know how lucky he was. He now had the best Mother in the world. She increased the food s little bit. She let him drink the milk mostly. She said she feels his strength returning. She would hold her fingers to his neck.

I made mother lie down and sleep now. She slept for about two hours. She got up and checked his hands and feet. She showed me where it was turning red. She said this isn't good. She fed him a little and made him sip milk. I could see the worry in her face.

Atsa came to us to see how he was doing. Mother said he needs a doctor to remove his toes and fingers. He said the roads weren't open yet. She said she would try but to get him here as fast as he can. Another day went by. Mother was at her wits end. She asked Atsa of peyote??? He said he had none of this. She asked me to check at the store to see what they had!! Atsa spoke of chinamen using a drug the whites call "heroin". She told Atsa to talk with the yellow men to see if they could help us with that. I returned from the white store embarrassed!! I told mother I failed at my task. Asta brought her the chainman's heroin. She put him to sleep with it chanting a prayer as she blew the smoke to his face. She asked me what took me so long to come back. I didn't answer her. She removed the fingers and toes before he became infected. She slowly brought him back to earth. Even when he was acting strange she just kept on smiling. After over three weeks in her care; the boy stopped asking for his Mother. I took over for her and demanded she sleep. She slept for an hour and checked on him. Then lay down to sleep again.

Mother took her station back. She was feeding him much more now. He was gaining his strength and she had him walking. About three steps at a time!! She would make him lye down and play her flute. She would get him up again and try walking. This is when the doctor finally arrived. He was "Astonished" He said he ought to be dead. He asked who did this for him??? We all turned and looked at Mother!! She said "Yah-the-hey and took off out of the door. The doctor just couldn't believe it.

I went to our lodge and mother had the fire burning. Without a word we both just collapsed. Other then waking up cold; feeding the fire with wood. We slept for the next two days. The sun was in the sky this morning. What a site to be blessed. We had our first visitor this day. Atsa came to us smiling. He said the doctor waits to talk with us!! Mother said she has nothing to say!! I said "Mother" you're a hero in town. She looked at me and told me I was a legend. I knew what she meant. This made me sick, sad, and mad. I told her I would talk to the doctor. Atsa never heard of us. He didn't understand. I told him I would explain it to him on the way to town. $)**%%&(^^((&&^^&!!!!!!

I told Atsa the whole story. I told him of the blood, the broken bones. Sewing my mother's leg. I told him of the way we were hated; just because she is my mother. And I am her daughter. I said why cant the $&^&% people understand this. This made him laugh. He said he felt love for my mother and I. He laughed again; he said that knows the boy does too!!! I asked if he would look over the boy? He said like you I am an Indian. I was crying again. I told him it isn't fair. He said no it's not. He said he couldn't change people's minds for them. He said the boy was asking where we were. I was just walking and thinking. I pulled my flute from my back. I played the song of need for the water, as we walked. Then I had an idea!!! I asked him if Hanyauk was in town. He said he just got there this morning. I told him I had more fun working for him then anything I have ever done. He said do you know a different Hanyauk!!! I laughed and said he's loud and crazy but a real nice man, and he could use some help. He said he would talk to him after I see the doctor! I told him to send the doctor home. I said we don't need any more legends. I just wanted to talk to Hanyauk.

I went straight to Honyauk. Atsa brought him out of the saloon. He was cyi-yien and carrying on. He lifted me up and spun me around. He was so happy to see me. I was thinking this will kill him when I tell him why I'm here. It took a long time to tell him of this. I made him mad. I was crying and the last thing I asked of him was to meet with the boy. He waved me off and returned to the saloon. I ran back to Mother. Mother told me not to cry. She said the spirit told her let him go with the wind. I told her of the town people that felt bad for him but that none of them stepped forward to help us with this. She started playing her flute. She stopped and told me she has looked at our journey so far. She said; "we are hated by the white and the red". She said the only reason we were accepted in this town was because they needed us. She said now that were done they will look at us and not the boy. She asked me if I felt their love when she sent me to town for our needs!! I laughed. I told her of the fight I got into in the general store with the lady who works there. I told her that this was when you were first tending the boy and you asked for something to ease his pain. I told her Atsa was asking you of the "Laudanum" that the whites use, and I ran to the store to see if I could buy it!!! Mother said I don't remember you bringing this to me!! I chuckled and told her, "No" that I didn't. I told her next of the trade. I said I showed her the bright shiny knife that the wagon train people gave me. I said she looked like a coyote with one leg caught in a trap. I learned later that she thought I was threatening her with the knife, and I really did feel bad for her after this. Mother said; "what did you do" with concern in her voice!! I yelled at mother that I was "Scared"!!! Tee Hee. I told her I pulled her dress up over her head and hung her from the ceiling. Mother said; may the Great Spirit help you my daughter. I told her of Atsa telling me she was too embarrassed to talk of this with anyone. We both started laughing with no control of our selves. Yup. Those were the days!!! We moved on. We spent the summer just traveling the land. Most of the wars were over now. Except for the wars with "US" I told mother I was much more comfortable around the red men. She told me they are a "conquered Nation". She told me felt the "Spirit" leaving them.

We were in the timber above the lake of the Coeur d Alene on the East side of it. We fashioned a hut out of mud and branches of the cedars and made ready for winter to come. She told me of the trade with the white men that the local tribe does here, and that we will be noticed before long. She told me not to do more then to hold my defensive posture when it happens. She made me promise her!!! She told me of their wisdom when dealing with the whites to trade furs of the animals.

This is where I met "Lomasi" (which is pretty flower) She was from a tribe to the south of us. Her man was a fur trapper who was a French Man. She had much Love for her man, and the Spirit to show this for him. My Mother Lozen had me talk with her. She had a bright Spirit about her. She told me of her tribe trading her to the trapper for two horses. She talked of her love growing like the Aspen trees for the man that she called "Luke" She told of two children she gave him that still walk this earth. Mother left me with her as she left for a few days to talk with the tribe of Lomasi.

Lomasi took me hunting with her. We were hunting birds to make a feast for Luke who was to return from his trapping lines along the lake. We used our "slings" to hunt the birds. We had more fun doing this then I could remember. I felt the freedom for the first time to hunt without worry about being watched by the army or the tribes. We dressed the grouse and put them on the fire. Lomasi used herbs and spices and wrapped the birds in the bark to cook them. It was delicious to eat. I asked her of her children? She told me of the Mission at Cataldo. She sent them there to learn the ways and talk of the white men.

When Luke returned; Lomasi ran to greet him, and I felt his Love for her too!!! Luke was a happy man. Luke called me "Rachel" Because he couldn't pronounce my name. I helped Lomasi tan the hides for the following week. Luke kept us with water and wine to pee on the hides for tanning. We were quite "Giddy" as we drank and peed on the hides. It was fun!!! Luke would laugh and encourage us to drink. As we were scraping the hides Mother came home. I had a headache and didn't want to talk with her. Lomasi explained the problem to Mother Lozen. Mom just laughed at me. I stuck my toung out at her.

We moved along the lake for the next few days. I told Mother Lozen of what I had learned from Lomasi. I asked her of the "Funny" noises they made at night. I described the noise as that of pain that made her Happy!!! Mother just smiled and told me I was learning. I didn't understand this!!! But I was about to learn of this!!!

After the sun rose to the sky ten times, I was fishing in the lake. I saw two canoes traveling towards me. There were two men in each canoe. I picked up my catch and watched them. I was wondering what this would bring to us. As I was cooking our fish over the fire. I felt the presence of others around us. As I looked to mother who was playing her flute, I saw it in her eyes, her notice of this too. I stood to my feet and shouted "Yah teh hey" and held my lance to my side. Three warriors of the Coeur d Alene were coming out of the brush and joined mother at the fire. She finished her song. She then asked them to join us. I added more fish to the fire as mother talked with them. The warrior that was near my age, asked me of the color of my hair. I asked him what difference it makes weather a bear is black or brown. He said it makes no difference, but that I was Beautiful. I saw a face that I trusted and sat to talk with him. I asked him what he sees "Beautiful" in me. He told me of the spirit of the "Lozen" that's spoken of in his tribe. That I was the one who sent the man with crooked fingers home to his tribe of the Crow. He told me the Crow warrior that he met described me, as "beautiful" I told him of the Crow Warriors wish to take the life of Xa'Xiats from the mother Lozen. He then talked of the other Crow warrior that came to their camp. The warrior told a story of the yellow haired spirit of a Bear. He said he feels a "Legend" in front of him. I then took the flute from my back and played the song of the owl, as the fish cooked over the fire. He asked of the sub chief I marked with shame. I told him he probably deserved it. I asked him to ask no more questions. I returned to my song with the flute. Mother Lozen then joined the tune with me and the men sat and listen. We ate our dinner and the men invited us to their reservation on the other side of the lake. Mother Lozen asked why they wanted us to gather with them. The tall older one said it will be a favor to the Great Spirit should we do this. She asked if the whites were there on their land. He said only at the front of the reservation, that they didn't want their spirit to enter their lands. Mother told him she would give this much thought before she answers him, and asked not to make it known to the white men we are here. He bowed his head to mother and said its not to be spoken of. As they were leaving I gave one sharp clear note from my flute. My friend turned and smiled at me and I was thinking? I wonder where the fourth man was?? He just smiled and walked out of site. Mother Lozen just raised her eyes at me. She thanked me for not talking of the Legend. This made me laugh. I told her it's like having a curse and a blessing at the same time!!!

Mother Lozen then renewed our practice with the staffs and wrestling. She told me she just does this to keep our bodies strong so we can face a challenge. She said I was ready for the battle to come; but I need to learn to live now. She said I was "cheated" from this part of my life!!! This went on for a week with the sweat on my brow. I asked her of it one evening. She told me of taking me from the wagon. She told me of what the Great Spirit had told her of this. She said she was hated by women of the tribe for this, and told to be ready to defend us from them. I asked why they have hate for me?? She said it's the color of my hair and my skin. She told of him asking her to Love you or leave you. I understood this but still couldn't see why the hate. She asked me this night if I sensed someone?? I told her of the fourth man that came in the canoe. I looked to her eyes and told her he's not more then fifty feet away. She picked up her flute and said bring him to me. And she started to play the song of the Bear. I picked up the cast iron skillet and banged it over the fire. I then yelled that I was going to wash it. She nodded her head and kept playing her flute as I disappeared in the forest. I came around back of the warrior and nailed him over his head. I grabbed his collar and drug him to mother, and started to clean the pan. She thanked me and went back to playing her flute. After near an hour the warrior awoke, and he sat there rubbing his head. Mother asked him of the Chief of his nation, she asked how many wives that he has. The warrior looked down in a code of silence. He refused to answer this. I slapped his back with my lance and encouraged him to answer. He sat there ready to die. Mother Lozen then took her knife from the sheath and described a white mans neck tie to him.(which is to split the toung and stretch it over his chin) He suddenly found the words in his mouth. It turned out that he had six wives. Mother was shaking her head up and down and told him this is good. He put his hand behind his back to steady himself, and I kicked it out from under him. I didn't want him getting comfortable. She asked him a few more Questions and told him to go!!! As he was leaving mother told me that the Chief follows the old ways. I didn't have a clue what she was talking about. But I was to learn of this. We spent the rest of the winter by the lake. She spoke of the sacred number "Seven" She felt the time was right!!!

It was now early summer when a warrior came to our camp. He told of the chiefs asking why we hadn't accepted his invitation to join him. Mother Lozen told him she feels the hate of the women of their nation, she said that it boils like cooking a stew. The warrior offered her protection from this. She said "NO" that we didn't need their protection, that we will arrive with our weapons sheathed, but we will deal with it with no help. She said if they wish to see our blood run that we will take them to the edge of a cliff. Then ask him again if they still wish this. The warrior said this is not normal but gave her his word that they will not help us. He then said the legend is true!!! Mother said we would be there by the next moon. She told me of speaking with the tribe of Lomasi. She said they told her of the Chief of the tribe. She said they made her feel his Spirit. She said the Great One smiled on her face.

We bathed our bodies and combed our hair. We tied the feathers to our hair in a ceremony of playing the flute while the other placed the feathers. Mother Lozen asked if I were ready for this. I felt the strength she had shown me rise with my blood and nodded yes to her. I have to admit it; She was a beautiful woman!!! We walked to their reservation with pride on our faces as the people started to gather. I felt a stone hit me in the back and instantly went to a defensive posture. Mother was at my back as the stones continued we were stopping the stones with our staffs. She raised her hand to the crowd and brought them to quietness. While holding her staff she used her foot and staff to group six of the rocks together. She then shouted to the women and told them to send six of their best to do battle. I felt my back touching hers as she shouted this, never letting my guard down for a second. They sent six women to the front of themselves with sheathed staffs like ours. Mother quietly told me to take the two larger women to my task, and she would handle the four of them.

The battle didn't last long. I had the two at my task on the ground. Mother had sent two to the ground and was still fighting with two of them; and I struck one so hard that her feet went out from under her and mother took the last one to the ground. The last one lifted her self from the ground and was now standing. She threw her staff to the ground. Mother Lozen then thanked them for the battle and asked if this is where it ends?? The last woman shouted to the rest of them to give their promise that this is where it stops. They all cast their staffs to the ground. My heart was beating at the speed of the drums as the women walked away. I now understood her talk of "Hate" The Chief and my friend now approached us and asked us to sit with them for a feast. The women brought us bowls of fresh water to wash our faces. They looked down from us as they offered this to us. Mother Lozen told her woman tending her to look up into her eyes. I nodded the same to the one tending me, and waited for her to speak. She simply said she wished to call them sisters!! She said we need no honor for this. She said again. "Sisters" We feasted on venison this evening. My friend sat by my side. He asked me if I were trying to become a legend again! with a smile on his face. I told him I was the Xa'Xats A warrior, that its up to the Lozen if what he tells me is true. There was much talk of happiness; as the men admired our bodies. The six women took us to the river. They washed us and prepared us for the ceremony of "joining". As I was standing there naked; the one washing me pointed to a young warrior who was watching me. She told me of making love to him. She told me of his tender ways. The women were all happy and laughing now. I told the one with me that I have never done this before. She told me of breaking my "Curtain" and suggested I pick the young one watching us. She gave me great praise for the fight that we won. She promised to help me when I was done. I was now in the gaze of many men of the tribe. Some of them were showing me their penis. I told the girl helping me, that I had seen the rabbits do this!! She just Laughed and told me that most of the men are like rabbits, to choose her favorite!! I watched as Mother Lozen walked away with the chief of the tribe with only a glance at me from her steel gray eyes, I took the friend of my helper's hand and followed him to his lodge. I stopped him and told him I have never done this before!! He promised me"Gentleness" if I would like to try!! My helper was smiling and nodded her head to me and into his tent we went!!! "I didn't know what to expect"

He was genital but it hurt me. As I held him next to my body; he held me and kissed me, and turned me to him. He looked to my eyes. He said it would become easier now that my curtain was broken. I now felt no love for him and lye down to sleep. I lay awake all night. I finally took my flute and played the song of the coyote as I sat there thinking. I left his lodge in the morning. My helper was outside the door. With a sad face she took me to the river and washed me. I told her I feel no love for him. She asked if I were done? I said yes and asked her to leave me.

I took my belongings with me to a spot near the Chiefs tent and stayed there alone at night. This lasted for a week. I hadn't spoke with my mother yet and longed to hear her voice. I was deep in my sleep when I felt mother shaking me. She was packed and ready to go. With her head she motioned to the canoes, and I gathered my gear and we left. We returned to our camp on the east side of the lake, and we packed up all that we needed. Three days had passed since we left the camp of the Chief, and he sent a runner to talk with Lozen. She told the runner to return to the Chief with a message. That if she is with a male child she will show this to him. But she demanded two spirited appaloosa horses, a bear hide, and the sacred feathers of the chickadee if she would keep her promise to him. The runner then nodded and left us. She then spoke with me of our "minstrel cycles". And of how she knew I was safe. She said I was fourteen now and she didn't want me to be with a child till I have learned what Love is. She told me I had started this journey now with my first man, and asked if I "Love" him. I told her "NO" that I don't. I told her I had feelings for him that disappeared after he hurt me. She said I had my first lesson and that I had learned. At the time I had only figured out that it hurt!! We played our flutes as we waited. When we finished I asked if she had Love for the Chief? She just smiled and spoke of the need for a brother or a sister to me, who can help protect the Bear. She told me of the hate for us, that it would stick in the lips of our mouths like honey. Before returning to her flute she added that we needed horses to complete our journey. I looked at her and thought. Well, that kind of makes sense!! I made Mother promise to never do this again. She nodded to me and played the song of the Coyote. I threw a rock at her. She laughed and looked at me. #$^3%#%%$ warrior woman.

The tribe sent us two beautiful horses and a quiver of arrows for each of us. The warrior unfolded the bear hide. It was so soft that it took me back home to the cave. I treasured it more then anything in this world. We had received the sacred feathers, and they were beautiful. They were attached to strings of leather with beading that surrounded them. Mother instantly put them in my hair. The one in charge asked where we were going too?? Mother just smiled at him and told him to follow the legends and he will find us. She returned to playing her flute. I noticed the man who, How do I say this? He had taken me! #%^%&#^ And went to talk with him. I told him I feel empty. That I had fooled myself with love. His face turned sad as he rode away. I felt bad for telling him this. But I felt pride in being honest. We left early the next morning riding to Post falls where we set up our camp.

My horse was a stallion and would throw me from his back whenever we rode. Mother Lozen then showed me of making him a Gelding by removing his testicals. He settled down after this. We rode wide around Fort Sherman to avoid the soldiers. Mother told me that they ask questions that she has no answers to give them. I was starting to understand this. We were away from the people whom worked at the mill, and let our horses graze. We followed the river fishing it to the mill in Spokan. It had a small lumber mill and a few whites and a few Indians that tended it. Mother had shown me Fort Sherman that sat near the river. She told me of the trust that she holds for the fort. She told me of speaking with a Captain from the fort. She said he uses many words when he talks. She said, don't let the words confuse you. She said to look him in his eyes. She told me of how the treaty was struck with the Spokan's to keep peace, and of how she felt safe here near the fort. Mother Lozen told me about the treaty, and that if we stay by the river we are safe. She told me of growing up here. She told me to talk with the whites if they offer this. She told me they are not all bad, to get to know them. We started to fish for our dinner and mother moved downstream and I moved up. I set a string net in the river and fished with my pole as I waited for the net to fill. I was dropping my line in a hole when I noticed the bird's flutter and fly. I pulled my lance near me and waited for a bite. I felt the eyes of another watching me; I felt no threat at the moment. I finally turned to see who was watching, and saw a young cowboy with his hat in his hand. He was white but didn't propose a threat to me. He wore no weapons; I had never been this close to someone my age and of my color that was alive before; as he walked to me holding his hat. He had long brown hair and a smile on his face. He started talking as he was near me now. I didn't have a clue what he was saying. I stepped closer to him and felt his face. I was astounded. His smile grew large as I did this; and I panicked! And I ran. I turned and saw him still smiling and ran and ran and ran. I came to Mother Lozen and told her what happened. She looked at him and was laughing at me, and I didn't understand this. She took me by the hand and led me back to the boy, using hand language as she talked she asked him to join us for dinner. I was staring at him, and reached and touched his face again. He slowly took my hand and held it to his face. I wasn't scared anymore. The boy sat with us as I was cleaning the fish and mother was playing her flute. I was serving him dinner he took my hand and I felt his face. I was ready to run when his smile settled me. I smiled back and we ate our fish. He sat with us till it was near dark listening to Mother and I play our flutes. He got up to leave and reached out with his hand, and I took it as he gently squeezed it. I smiled at him and watched as he walked, and turned to Mother Lozen and asked her why she invited him to eat with us??? She told me of her sister living here where the whites are friendly and it was time for me to see this. She told me I would have to ask myself if I were white?? Or red?? She went back to her flute and left me confused.

I went to the river the next day and washed my clothing and my body. My mother reached into her bag and threw me a bar of soap. She was standing there telling me how to use it, and laughing at me as I went. When I was done she was brushing my hair asking me of my minstrel cycle. I said "MOTHER LOZEN" and blushed to the color of an apple. She said you never know when that might be a handy thing to keep track of it. I told her that it hurts. She told me it gets easier as time moves along. She next reminded me of getting pregnant when this is done!! I said ^%$% Mother, and didn't want to hear anymore. She finished tying the feathers in my hair and said listen to me now!! You never know when your heart will wake up! With a sound, with a feeling, or a song. She tapped on my nose with her finger and went to her flute. It was sunset over the river when I went to the edge and looked at myself in still stand of it. I didn't know if I were looking at a warrior or a princess with my hair done so nice. When I returned to camp Mother had a large dinner about ready, I asked her who is coming tonight. She just smiled and shook her head. Within ten minutes of asking, the boy came to camp with a loaf of bread. I was still dressed in a wrap waiting for my cloths to dry and much of my body was exposed to his view. He removed his shirt and put it on me and sat down and talked to mother. After we ate Mother picked up her flute and played it. The boy and I were talking in sign and spoken language and getting nowhere. He tapped on his chest and said, "Ken Asher", I copied his speech and called him Kenasher!! He said that works!! He did this several times. It popped into my head and I tapped on my chest and said Xa'xats several times. The blanket slipped as I did this exposing my breasts. Kenasher reached out and covered me. He then laughed and called me ezactos when he couldn't pronounce the name. Using a stick I drew a picture of a bear and looked back at him. My mother was laughing uncontrollably now and said she was going to lay down and sleep. He looked at me and said "Little blond bear" with a smile on his face. It went on this way till late in the evening. He drew a picture of the mill up the river from us and I figured out that it was his father that ran it. He pointed to the picture he had drawn of his father and rubbed out the mother, he tapped on his chest?? I shook my head and rubbed out his father in the picture!! We were both missing a parent in our lives. He put his arm around me and held me. He next handed me my flute and asked me to play it. I played the soft song of the birds as he put his hands behind his head and listen. This went on for a time. He finally got up and pointed to the mill and said some words. He was looking at me smiling and said a few more words. He then stepped to me and placed his lips on mine and smiled and walked away. My blood was on fire. He was about thirty feet away when I blew a single high note!! He turned and looked at me smiling at him and waved goodbye. I took off his shirt and ran it to him. And I looked at his curious smile!!! He just shook his head and went home. I started to "shiver" as I watched him.

I had never had feelings like this and ran to my mothers lodging and shook her awake. I asked her to explain "Love" to me??? She had a look on her face like her pants were too tight when she reached for her flute. She gave a twirl of notes and asked if my heart felt like this?? I put my hand on my heart and felt it beating and told her "Yes" She just pulled up her covers and said your learning and went back to sleep. I lay there the rest of the night thinking about it. I just didn't know!!!

I asked her the next day if it was because he has the same color skin as I do??? She took out her knife and slashed my arm, not deeply, but the blood started to run. She looked at me and told me, His blood, My blood, and the blood of every man and woman on earth has red blood. She had a way with words!! And with a knife too!! Ouch!!!

We were riding the horses now looking for my aunt Kumbah. We saw a detachment of Calvary riding to the fort. Mother Lozen was looking at them when she told me that if we ever wind up being there, they will ask many questions. She said to tell the truth of what they ask me unless I don't want to answer. She told me to say nothing if I am faced with this. We spoke to a few of the local tribe of Spokan Indians, and we were directed to the fort. They told us of the lists that they keep for a census on the tribes. We went back to our lodging and the boy Kenasher was waiting for us. Mother Lozen asked me to get him to help us and went to her lodging. I was trying to explain to him that I was looking for aunt Kumbah!! I thought he didn't understand the name was female. I drew a picture of a man with his hardware sticking out and a picture of a woman without the hardware!! I was tapping on the female as I looked at his face. He was turning the color of a ripe red apple!! I smacked him for that!! And we both started laughing. I rolled my eyes at him and pointed at my picture. Between pointing back and forth from the picture to mother he said its your "AUNT KUMBAH" that your looking for!! I gave him a kiss. He was now rolling his eyes at me!! So I smacked him!!! I had never had this much fun in my whole life. And he was hansom.

We went on with our talking till near dark while lying on my bear hide. Kenasher then got an Idea in his head and was pointing at the mill and said he would be right back. I was looking at him like he was crazy as he was spilling his words and walking away from me. He stopped still looking at me and came back and gave me the kiss of my life. He then ran shaking his finger at me to the mill. I thought, I like the way he kisses me. I was picking up the dishes to wash them when he came back with an Elder. The elder explained to me that he worked for the boy's father as an interpreter. I told him of asking Kenasher of my aunt Kumbah. He laughed and said "Ken-Asher" I asked (Alah-moot) what the two names meant?? He shrugged his shoulders and told me to call him "Ken" I said it a few times and he stood by me proudly with a smile on his face. He told me like the rest of them; we had, go to the fort!!! I told him of talking with Mother Lozen about this and I don't want to bring problems down on my mother for any reason in the world. He asked how this mother and daughter came to be. I told him she found me in the prairie wandering with the wind, and that's all I will say. He took a long look at me and asked if I was the white warrior that left the red warrior with a crooked hand?? I looked at him and said nothing!!

He then turned to Kenasher and talked with him for a bit. When it was done he said he will help me with this. Kenasher said he wanted to see what they could do to help us! I thanked him for his help.

The next day I started tugging on Kenasher's arm to go fishing with me. He was telling me he had to work!! I didn't really understand what work was but I was pissed off!! I turned my back to him. His face was peeking over my shoulder with a smile as big as the sun!! I said %%$%^*^^to him. He looked into my eyes till I forgave him; and let him return. Well. After a looooooong kiss I let him go. I was terrible.

Two days had passed when Kenasher came back to me with Ala-moot. They still wanted us to go to the ^#$#$#^% Fort. He told me to use my strong face when I speak. I told Alah-moot that I wasn't good with talking, that I get my words wrong. He said, "Me too" We brought mother with us and went to the office of the Captain. I was scared just being in the building. I felt short of breath. The Ala-Moot introduced us to the captain. His eyes were looking at mother. I turned and saw her smiling. She said she leaves this to her daughter; and the questions began. Very first thing he asked about was Mother and I. I told him of growing up along the trail. He looked to mother and said he looked for her. he spoke of the land of Yellowstone. Mother told him she waited. She asked that he talk to me. I felt the tension between them. I asked of my Aunt Kumbah. He knew nothing of mother's sister. He tried to speak with mother again! She started softly playing her flute. I stepped in front of him and asked again of Kumbah. He said I have no manners. I told him I wasn't there to discuss my *)^&*)^^ manners. The Captain then pulled a second book from his desk and asked me to sign my name to that book. I asked Ala-moot, "why" he uses a different book for me? He said because I am "White" The captain then told him he wants my "Christian" name. Alah-moot explained to me of following the Bloodline of my family. I thought that's easy! I took my knife from its scabbard and slit my finger. I then pressed it into his book. I thought the roof would fall in. He talked of honesty. I told him with honesty that I didn't know of my parent's linage to me. I gave him my blood!! They were acting crazy! I asked if he needed more blood? The Captain gave up. I told him that I was raised by Mother Lozen, and of my pride in this union. I told him of being named "Xa'xats" by my Mother. He asked Mother if this was correct. She smiled and said the words came from my mouth, and she has never heard me lie. I told him that she is all I have ever known. That if he wishes me to sign my name to a book, that I will be listed as a member of the tribe of the Lozen.

The Captain next went to my mother and asked her where I came from? She talked of the parries where the buffalo once roamed. She said she heard my Spirit call out to her from the wind. She then played the song of the wind on her flute. She looked up at him. And asked if he had seen any buffalo wandering the parries in the large herds that once traveled the land. "He said no" She finished the song. She looked at him and said, "Like the dry bones of the buffalo" that she sees her tribe!!! She said the spirit of the "Tonka" is what travels this land now. She said like the buffalo that gave suck to their young; that she did this for Xa'xats. She said my spirit was wandering. She said it wandered to "ME"

With a look of disgust he pulled out his book and started to look for Kumbah's mark next to her name. He had me sign this book. Ala-moot and Kenasher helped me with this. It was the first time I had ever seen my name, "Xa'xats". I did this with great pride. Kenasher stood behind me and guided my hand. I wore my proud face.

The Captain found three Kumbah's. He told us that they were all assigned to the reservation in Colville, and that was a year and a half ago. This made me happy to hear this. I went to the Captain and kissed his cheek. For the first time I saw him smile.

As we were leaving mother stood before the captain and played revelry for him and smiled at him as she left. I stopped Alah-Moot and had him tell the Captain that I felt the spirit of Tonka that my mother spoke of this day! That we came here with hope in our hearts. I told him that if he pursues his path to my white parents!! That I see a herd of buffalo that will trample his grave. He stood with a smile; saying I understand this now.

The Captain asked Mother to talk with him in privet. She said she would just be a minute. They stood and talked for a time. She gave him a passionate kiss. I still didn't understand their way of thinking. But I enjoyed seeing the kiss. I asked mother Lozen this night if the Captain was part of her life. She suddenly smiled and said that was long ago.

She told me of his protecting her. She said she mistook the love he showed her. Still smiling, she asked that we not speak of this again. I thought, "Wow" Mom sure knew her way around!!!

I was crying the next morning. Mother asked what this is about? I yelled that I don't know how to talk to anybody!! She said to tone my voice down or she would shut my mouth for me!! I told her I was sorry, but she never taught me of this. She said she didn't see much talking yesterday while I was lying on the bear hide kissing Kenasher!!! I smiled as I thought about this. She shook her finger at me and reminded me of my minstrel cycles!!! I told her the time was right, but he wouldn't do this for me, that he spoke to me of honor for me. She was shaking her head up and down, I was "Frustrated" She sat with me and talked of my encounter with the man of the tribes. She apologized for bringing me to him. She talked of the men looking at me. She said she wanted it to be my choice. She said she loves me and she is pregnant with a child. She said she wanted to see me protected should something happen to her. I saw her smile rising as she spoke of Kenasher. I asked her if my life will be like hers waiting for the Captain?? She reached out and touched my nose. And told me I am white. I realized that I had never thought about it that way before.

I decided to stop thinking about this. I got up the next morning and decided to go take a swim. Kenasher had brought me a big towel that I wrapped around myself. He told me to wear it unless I was in the water. I hung it in a tree and just swam. I felt better now. I grabbed the towel and walked back to camp. Kenasher was there talking with Mother. She was asking him to look over us if we go to Colville to find her sister. He agreed to do this for us without another thought. He looked at me and asked if I wanted to go swimming??? I threw the towel to my shoulder and said "YES" He turned as red as an apple. He then covered me with the towel. He said I told you when "your" in the WATER!!! I said oh.----He went back to the mill.---mother was shaking her head. She said I need work! I went back to the river for a swim. $$%^%&^%$

Mother had been gone from our camp for two days now. Kenasher said he saw her at the fort. He said she was making arrangements for He and the Captain to look over our safety and handle any business that may come while we were gone. He asked me not to worry about her. He told me that she's staying in the guest Quarters. I asked Ken to stay with me till my mother returns. This was the first time in my life I was alone and without her. Kenasher agreed to do this for me. I made him stay in my lodge. We talked this night of my mother. It was Kenasher that brought up the Captain. He said the Captain called him to his office. He said the Captain noticed the look in our eyes whenever our eyes met. The Captain told him to behave himself. He told him that I am an Indian. I asked him if he felt love for me? He said "yes" I asked him to hold me!! He smiled and said this is as far as it goes for right now. He said he promised the Captain. He asked me to give it time for our love to grow. I agreed. $$%$%$%%^ kind of. Mother returned the following day.

Mother was talking with a half-breed woman this morning when I returned from fishing. She was dressed in buckskins and she was a nice women. Mother said talk to her and got up and left. She had me sit with her. She explained the white mans way of thinking about the women, "that they learn to love". She said I know your going to think I'm coo coo but you have to hide your body and your feelings if you want to trap one of them. I told her of talking with the women on the reservation. I told her of how they share their men with the others!! She said I know, I know, I know. She said white men don't do that. I asked her "Why" She said if I figure that out to come back and talk with her!! I was really confused now. She told me to make sure that the "One" that I pick is the "One" you will spend your life on earth with. I told her honestly that I was trying to lure Kenasher in like a fish!!! She shook her finger in my face, and told me; Love is like fishing, just keep pulling him in. She said again to make sure he is the "One" She got up and left. I guess that makes sense!!

Mother was starting to get a "Bump" in her belly and she asked me to say goodbye to Kenasher and make ready to leave. I told her he was working at the fort delivering lumber to them. She smiled and told me to ride. I nearly rode my horse to death. I ran to Kenasher and held him. I told him I was near ready to leave him. The Captain was standing next to him and said it wont be forever!!! Kenasher asked me to wait for him to talk. The Captain took my hand and said he wanted to talk to me first. We stood under the Maple tree as he looked deep into my eyes. He told of talking with my mother. He said they mostly talked of me. He said he loves my mother, but that it wasn't meant to be. He talked of giving his promise to her; that he will watch over me if anything should happen to my mother. He talked of the troubles in Colville. He asked me to watch her like a hawk. I promised him I would do this. I was hunting for the words to use as we talked. I asked him why did he look for my mother? He smiled and said; "I Love her" He turned and walked away. I couldn't find the words?? DAMN IT!!!!

We were making ready to ride to Colville when Kenasher came to our camp. We had been talking long enough now that we understood each other, pretty much. I told him I was sorry that we couldn't, "make happy times", that my cycle was wrong to do this. He was blushing again, and I started crying. I was so pissed at myself for not knowing how to say this. He started laughing so hard that it ruined our kiss. I was stomping my feet and I smacked him. He finally stopped laughing and gave me a passionate kiss. Then rubbed his arm and said goodbye. I leaned down from my horse for a second kiss and told him that I picked him as the "ONE", He was shaking his head and I waved goodbye to him as we rode. Mother Lozen told me I need work!! I told her I don't need her @$%##@$^$ help anymore!!!. This upset her. She leaned forward on her horse in pain. I started crying and took her from the horse to help her. She asked me to use my flute and play the song of the birds; this made her settle down. I asked her where the pain was?? She tapped on her belly!!! I asked if she were sure she could ride?? She said its now or never. I held her and told her I was sorry. I was cursing myself for the words that I used. She told me she only trusts Kumbah with this. She said she was the "Seventh Daughter" of her family.

It took eight days to get to Colville. The stagecoach passed us twice. We fished from the river on our trip down there. We had cut throat trout the size of the river. Mother had spoken to me about Kenasher and told me to keep my pants pulled up on this trip. I agreed and took out my flute and played the happy songs as we went. I was thinking of him though.

We rode through the town of Colville. There wasn't much there. It had a small café and a general store. The buildings were placed too and fro. They had a big building that was a hospital. Mother spoke of the doctors of the whites. She showed me the fort where the soldiers lived. It was quiet here. I felt comfortable with it. We rode onto the reservation and mother talked with the people there. At one point the tribe gathered just to feel my hair. My blue eyes just amazed them; and the color of my hair astounded them. I felt no anger in them as we searched for Aunt Kumbah. A little girl ran to me with flowers; and I dismounted my horse. She had such a happy smile on her face that I just loved her. I dropped to my knees and asked her what her name was?? She giggled "Nalin" and reached and felt my face. I giggled and told her I was Xa'Xats, a warrior woman from the east. She "Growled" like a bear and hugged me. We were laughing with each other and having fun. I asked her to ride with me, that she could help me look for my aunt. Mother said, be careful now!! She was at my horse in a heartbeat, and I lifted her on and away we rode. She was showing her proud face as we rode. She told me she knows my aunt. Her mother was standing there with her hands on her hips, and a smile on her face. She told her you get down from there!!! Nalin got the "I'm Mad" look on her face and she started to cry. I told her mother she was helping me!! That I would bring her home when we were done. She was still laughing and just dropped her hand, and returned to her lodge. Nalin returned to her proud face and pointed the way. I was still young. It made feel lonely to ride with her. I felt I needed a daughter or a sister. She took us to the front of the lodge of Kumbah. I lifted her down from the horse. She was just fussing that the ride was over with a frown on her face now. I told her to show me her proud face. That I wanted her to tend to our horses. I had her hold up her hand and promise to do this for me. There was pasture next to the lodge. That little girl was a tugging and pulling and took the horses to pasture and just loving them to death. I was afraid she would be trampled, so I asked her to take me fishing. She was such a happy little thing, that it was a side of life that I had never known. It didn't matter what we talked about. Her bright little smile shown like the sun. We were lying on our sides talking, when she came up with an idea to make us sisters. She took my knife and poked her arm. She then got her tough face on and poked mine. She held her arm to mine and pronounced us as, "Sisters" I just loved her like no others. We caught a nice string of trout, and I told her to go play.

I was watching her when I heard mother shouting to me to come and meet Kumbah. I waved good-bye to Nalin and turned to meet my aunt.

I was "shocked" !!! She was short and overweight. I looked down at her as mother introduced her to me. Kumbah grabbed me and was holding me as I looked over her head and mouthed silently to mother "This is Kumbah" I should have been raised around others. My mouth keeps getting me in trouble. Mother told me later she was her half sister that she grew up with. I said "OH" and shut my mouth. We set up our lodging there on the reservation. Nalin saw us working and came to help. Using cedar bows we thatched it together. I chased mother off to visit with Kumbah; and Nalin and I finished it at just about dark; we stood by the river looking at the stars. It was so clear that I looked to the end of them. I asked the great spirit to teach me to talk. That I trip on my toung when I try!!! I was about to become sixteen now and my blood is moving with wants and don't wants traveling my brain. I saw a shooting star and made a wish on it before it disappeared, I was desperate for help with this. I told him of learning to fight, that I was ready for that. I told him I have a better chance of stopping a herd of stampeding buffalo!!, That I need a chance to use the words.

Nalin was laughing as I prayed. She said she says prayers for her father. That he's a mighty warrior from her tribe. That he rode with Chief Joseph the chief of her nation, and she thinks he's gone now. I gathered her to me and held her as we looked to the stars. I told her of loosing my parents to the Great one. I asked her if she knew her father? She said "no" that she was new born when he left. I told her it was the same for me. She told me her mother says this happens for a reason. I told her my mother tells me the same. She asked if I miss them. I told her of Mother Lozen making me honor them. And of how she raised me to be a warrior. I said I honor my mother with all my heart. That I believe she is the reason that I live. That I just have no memory of anyone else but mother Lozen. She hugged and kissed me and ran on home.

I was looking down the river at an aged woman who was walking my way. She came to me smiling dressed in her buckskins, and she was white like me. She started to talk to me in English, and I thought I'm not going to try this. I just shook my head to her no! She studied my face and asked me in the Sahaptian language what my name is?? I was ready to fall over, and told her "Xa'Xats" and asked her what hers is?? She told me "Annie" and went on to tell me of her home on onion creek. I asked her what she was doing here in Colville?? She told me of a tribel Elder that passed his spirit to the Great one that he helped her out in her time of need. I felt so alone that I told her I was going through my time of need in my life. She sat with me and asked me to tell her of this, I felt instantly comfortable with her and told her of my lack of knowledge to talk. She told me to talk with my beautiful eyes, that they say more then any words can ever say. She reached down and picked up my flute and asked me to play it for her. I was playing the soft tune of the lonesome coyote with my eyes shut, thinking of "Kenasher" as I played. When the tune was done I looked every which way!! And she was gone!!

Mother and Kumbah were now walking to me and I turned and saw them walk in. Kumbah instantly made comment on my beautiful blue eyes and she just sighed with a jealousy that made me smile. She then charged me and held me and rocked me with a quiet love. And I hugged her right back and told her I love her. She didn't want to let go. I asked her of "Annie" did you see her when you were walking?? She said she lives in all our hearts here on the reservation. She said that it's been years since she has been here from onion creek. I told her I just talked to her!!! She was still holding me smiling and said we all talk to her every day!!! I was confused. I shut my mouth and smiled on her. I realized she was right!! Say it with my eyes. I took to my flute and played the rest of the song I had started, with mother Lozen following my lead. Kumbah wished us goodnight and returned to her lodge. I told Mother of what Annie had told me. She just said; "she is right"!! And turned to her bed. I yelled at her and told her I have five cut-throat trout frying in the pan, don't you want to eat before bed?? She said she was tired and crawled into bed.

I sat there eating the trout thinking of Kenasher and there has to be better days ahead!!! Before I realized it I had eaten everything but a bite of the fish. My stomach was talking to me and I had the "TOOTS" I thought it will get better. I took my cloths to the river and washed them, and hung them on a branch to dry all night, as the evenings were still warm. I went naked to our lodging because it was dark out now. I liked to sleep naked because I loved the feel of the Bear fur when I snuggle into it. OH wow, was that a mistake. My better day, started with a pain in my belly at around five in the morning. I had to POOP!! I ran what I could to the horse pasture to do my business. As I was, well,,, releasing the pressure on my bowls, the mare of my mothers walked to me and snorted. I told her to go away!! She shoved me with her nose and I wasn't done yet, I screamed at her to "Go Away". I was almost done when she whacked me with her head, and knocked me over in my poop. I had grabbed a rag to wipe with, but had lost it in the rush. I was standing there naked. Covered in poop. And crying. The sun was just starting to peak over the hill when I ran back to the lodge and was looking for the soap. Mother then woke up and thought she smelled something. I was now crying saying; I cant finned thuuhhh soooap. She said may the great spirit help you girl, its in my bag, and buried her head. I grabbed a full wrap and headed for the river. I hung the wrap on a limb and wade slowly into the river. I was cursing that horse with every piece of my body that I scrubbed. The horse was standing there watching me as I cursed her. I finally got all the poop off of me and started to leave the river. The horse was sniffing my wrap and I yelled at her to get out of there. She did. With my wrap in her mouth she took off with the wind. I was crying again. My cloths were further down the river and probably not dry yet. The men were up now as I ran past them as fast as I could. I got a few whistles as I dove into our lodging. I was crying so hard now that I was out of control. Mother got up, she said I'm not even going to ask. She went to Kumbah's lodging and left me there, alone, and, crying. I was saying, there has to be better days ahead!!! I finally stopped it. And just said---"Oh crap" What will I wear now. My clothing was still hanging on a tree by the river. If the horse hasn't found it. I went back to bed.

Late in the after noon a warrior brought my clothing to me. As I reached for them he whistled at me and gave me a wink. &%$^&^^ warrior &^$%%@

Mother Lozen started to have problems already. She was around half way there, and it didn't look good. We borrowed a wagon and took her to the doctor in Colville. The doctor blamed her life style of being a warrior woman for the damage to her womb. I knew what he was talking about. I had our interpreter ask him what we should do?? He said defiantly don't travel back to Spokane. We had to pay the doctor. The tribe had nice people in it. They put together enough money to telegraph Spokane that we wouldn't be returning till the baby was born. I sent a message to Kenasher because he was looking over us, and mother didn't want trouble with the Coeur D Alene's. She was going to bring Kumbah back with us to help her and she was from the Spokan area originally. She was crying too and I felt helpless. I had no white man money. We traded what we had to send the telegram. I was looking out the front and noticed the kids going to school. The brain started working again, and I asked Aunt Kumbah about it. She told me they teach the young English mostly, and that's what I needed. I drug her with me and after much arguing I was now a "Student" I was a little older then most!! But a student. I remember some of the words that Kenasher taught me. But figuring out how to put them together is what got me in trouble. I was anxious to learn and the first week I was in school I drove everyone crazy with my practicing on them. They tried to teach me math. I didn't get it. I just worked on my English. Aunt Kumbah and Mother didn't know what I was saying. I used Nalin to practice on. Nalin brought a half-breed boy with her who could read and write in English. He was a huge help with this. He was mostly "shun" from the tribe and I knew how he felt about this. His name was (Enapay) which is "Brave". He would teach me if I played the flute for him. He told me of working for the café in town. He told me of a job washing the dishes. He was fired for fighting with a customer. He was tired of being called a half-breed. I told him of Honyauk. I knew exactly how he felt. I told him of the comments that were made about me behind my back. I apologized to him for the ways of my people.

He asked if this comes from the red or the white? I told him "both". I rushed home and told my mother of the job at the cafe.

Mother Lozen was talking to aunt Kumbah about the job. She said it's a white only kind of place, that they do hire Indian help when they work outside!! I begged Mother to let me try it, I promised her I would do my best!! She gave me permission to do this with one condition. She demanded that I start no trouble!! Tee Hee, I promised and I ran to the restraunt and applied. They had me washing dishes by the end of the day. I had to change my hours a bit to get my school to fit in there too. But the teacher was a nice lady who gave me extra help. I was figuring out quickly that it's to my advantage to be a Blue eyed Indian. Even though I had a dark tan. My skin is white. I spoke with Mother about this, and she was fine with it. She told me to use this as an "advantage" when I can!!!

I was leaving for school when I heard the deep rumble of a buffalo rifel up in the hills. I had heard this before, as mother and I traveled the parries. The people from the tribe were running for cover, I was looking for where it came from. I saw a man far away mounting his horse and he slowly rode away. Nalin ran to me crying and told me that it was Enapay that was shot!! She told me of the trade with the rancher on Gold Hill; and that he hired the buffalo men to do this. I asked her why he shot the warrior? She told me he was trying to be named as sub chief to the tribe!! I felt the Bear rise in my Soul and took Nalin home. I asked her Mother about this. She just gave me silence. I told her I understand this. I reminded her he was my friend. I asked that she tell me if she needs help with this. She nodded to me and took Nalin into her lodge.

It was just the teacher and I at school this day. She told me this was the second time this has happened. She was crying and said she had just got the kids to come back to school. I told her I would make them return. I asked if she had talked to the elders of this. She said she was white like me and they don't trust her. I told her I would speak for her, that I would take my Mother with me, that they honor her. She said they Honor me too, that they call me Tonka Xa'xats among the tribe. She knew of my mother having problems with carrying the baby. She next spoke of our "Legend" This made the fire burn in my eyes and my soul. I told her that it was different then the way she was told. I scolded her for listening to this trash talk. I firmly said she is my "Mother" and I will go to my grave to defend her from anyone who wishes to harm her. She started to laugh! She said she doesn't know of the man who is dumb enough to try to harm her!!! This made me laugh. She asked that I not get her involved in this. I thanked her for her wisdom; I was busy with school and work and never thought about anything but learning. The next day was the ceremony to honor the sub chief that gave his life for the tribes. The teacher asked to go home; she was too upset to teach this day. I told her I knew him. I asked her to stay till the Elder spoke over him. I told her I would walk her home. She just stood there and cried. I walked her home after the ceremony. I told her that I see his blood spilling to the ground. She saw the anger in my face and asked for a promise of no retaliation for this crime!! I was furious about this as I told her of his help and his friendship. She told me I might as well wear a target on my shoulders if I pursue this!! She was a lady of honesty. She reminded me that my mother comes, "First"!!! I forced myself to settle down.

I would wash the dishes and take them to the front. I would go out the back door and play my flute while waiting for the next load to be ready to wash. I was playing the song of the wolf one day, when a man who was half drunk stumbled in and sat with me. I was practicing my "English" on him and this made him laugh. He picked up his guitar and would sing a song a verse at a time till I sang it correctly. I would follow his lead with my flute as we did this each day. He would leave the singing to me when I learned the song, and play the flute as he taught me the words. We were having "Fun" and this went on for a month. The people from the café were spending more time listening to us out back then time they spent eating. This got the owner to thinking.

The owner of the restraunt finally gave up and had the restraunt built onto with canvas so he could have the music inside. I had my teacher show me how to introduce a song and we were the best act in town. Well!! We were the only act in town. The soldiers even came to hear us sing and play. The mans name that played the guitar was Bill. He had some experience with the music, and he would have me play for half the song and he would play while I sang for the rest of it. Since we were getting popular he asked about my name. He gave up pronouncing it and gave us a "Stage name" "Cinnamon Bear and Bill" The soft music that we played was the most popular with the customers. Along with school I was learning new songs. The soldiers would come in and sing to me and I would have Bill write the words down for practice while I put music to the song. I did all this by memory and Bill started teaching me the use of musical notes to add to the songs. I was fired from washing dishes and put my time into my songs. Bill was the head of this gang and demanded we be paid better. I left it up to him to handle the business and kept up with school too.

I was finally granted a council with the Elders. I was told that they risk their lives just to do this for me. It was late of night when we gathered in the center house. The head Elder asked for a blessing, and the council began. He talked of the warriors that moved up to Spokan for help with this. He told me they had no one to speak for the tribe. He spoke of the ranch on Gold Hill that held them hostage with the Buffalo guns. He spoke of the warriors that gave their life trying to stop this from happening. He asked that I not take any action on this, that they can't afford to loose any more men to the guns. I asked him if he had asked for help from the soldiers with the problem. He said that they sent him to the sheriff with this, that the sheriff is a good man but he is not allowed on the reservation unless it's a civil complaint. I asked him if they had tried this yet? He nodded his head and spoke of the man that was fell to the buffalo hunter. I told him I don't understand this. I told him of a Captain that I dealt with at fort Sherman. I gave him permission to use my name of "Tonka-Xa'xats" when they speak with them. I told him of Kenasher and Alah-moot who watch over us while we are here. I suggested they start with them. I told him of my "Love" for Kenasher. He told me I was wise, and asked me again not to get involved with the buffalo guns. I thought about this. I promised I wouldn't "Kill" them. His eyes came to me. I told him I fish the river and hunt the lands. If I were threatened by one of them; I would protect myself. He asked that I look over my new sister as I travel the rivers; He said her spirit is bright. He said she was Nalin-Yumni and he values her

Soul. I agreed. I told him I would give my life for my sister. He asked us to leave the center lodge one at a time. My blood was boiling with hate.

My little Nalin was upset with me. She told me all I do is work and sleep. Her mother was scolding her for her behavior. I told her mother its all right. I picked her up and told her she is right. I told her I have a chance to do something that I like to do. I then asked her to join me while I practice my songs. I asked that she would have to be quiet though. She gave me a hug so full of LOVE that it made me cry. I set up a chair to the side of the stage so she could watch.

The owner was mad at me for doing this. He said Indians are not allowed in the bar. I was looking at him thinking I was an Indian, and @&)&^# his rules. Bill helped me hang a blanket for her to sit behind where she couldn't be seen from the bar. She was quiet and bothered nobody. She was my little cheering section. When the bar was empty I sat her at the Piano. I just loved her so much.

I was crying one morning when I came to work. It was Saturday and I wanted my Mother to listen to me play and sing and she couldn't handle getting her in the bar. She was eight and months pregnant now and I was begging her to come!! The owner saw me crying and asked me what this was about. I told him of my Mother teaching me to play the flute, and of how she was better then me. He was staring at me and said he has an old wheel chair he will give her if she will play one song for him. I couldn't get that chair under her butt fast enough.

My school - teacher had prepared me to introduce the song of the Coyote and the Bear. I was to first tell them my name; "Xa'Xats" then give a brief history of the tale. I told her of my mother and how I wanted her to play the song. She suggested we both play it. She said I could drop in and out when I thought it was right. Bill taught me to do this with him and I had the day set. Mother Lozen was nervous, but I kept her calm. The people whom had heard of this now packed the doorways full. The owner shushed everybody and turned to Bill to begin.

Bill introduced Mother and I to the people giving emphasis on our names. I then spoke to the people and gave a brief history of the bear and the coyote. I was so proud to stand next to her. I filled my speech with pure Love. I nodded to Mother

She shut her eyes and the music started to drift through the building, filling every corner with its spirit. When she would hit a high note I would join in with her. You could feel it take you and drift your Soul down the river. As the notes left the mouth of my Mother, everyone felt it. The women were crying. I felt that they understood the Love of my Mother that I treasured in my heart. When Mother and I finished with both of us in tune. She opened her eyes to an astonished audience that just looked to her face.

Someone started clapping and by the time the people joined in from outside the building it nearly brought the roof down. Nalin couldn't stand it "no longer" and ran to my arms so proud. I was crying as Nalin and I held up my Mothers hand. The applause kept on coming, and we held her hands to the air!! And it got even louder as the crowd showed her their Love. We nearly had to call the Sheriff to handle the crowd when Kumbah wheeled Mother from the building. I started to play a new song and got the crowd back inside. The night went on with Bill helping me to play the music. With Nalin sitting beside me, the music went on. We were a hit. That was the last time Nalin was asked to sit behind the @#$%$#@$ curtain.

I was running to work so happy to go. When the boom of the buffalo gun sounded. I looked up the hill and saw him just sitting on his horse. He had shot a woman from the tribe. This was more then I could handle. I ran back to our lodge and grabbed my lance. Mother just nodded to me. I ran like the wind to the hills. I turned to north running as fast as I could, and spotted him just riding his horse. He was in no hurry. I took a station ahead of him and knocked him from his horse. With my lance at his throat he was showing fear. I made him lay face down in the dirt with his arms stretched out. I cut off the tendons to his right hand. He passed out from this. I made him a Gelding. I returned and went to work.

The following week Bill was teaching me about "Money" The owner had given us a raise in pay because we packed the building. Bill said he, himself was a "Drunk" and had no call to handle this for us. I told him I wanted enough of the white mans money to pay the hospital for Mother Lozen's baby. Nalin was there and asked him "Please mister Bill." He shook his finger in my face and told me that he was hanging by his teeth to not drink as we go through this. Nalin asked him to, please, wait a little longer, ---tee-hee--- and he growled like a bear. I said to her, "well you little devil" she giggled.

He had been sober long enough that his disposition was "Ruff" He demanded a piano player to add to the music; and he got one! She could only be there on Saturday though. The owner walked by me shaking his finger in my face!! Music must be something that either you have it!! Or you don't. He started to teach me to play the piano and I was astounded with the sounds. Bill had me, singing, playing the flute, and now with the Piano!! I suggested he teach little Nalin to play it; He had taught her to play the chords. He spread out her fingers and laughed as he did this, telling her she would be a fine pianist some day!!! I dropped out of school and treated the language, like a song. I was picking it up quickly with each new song that I sang. He told me I was ready and I begged him to stay. Just a little longer!! And the Bear was a growling. Nalin then looked him in his eyes. She said Mister Bill!!! will you be my Grandpa?? He swelled up with the pride of a Bear. I saw tears in his eyes as he accepted the honor. She was my secret weapon!!

I had been lucky with Bill. But it was Saturday night and he laid "Drunk" on the streets. I had brought Mother with me this night. The owner showed me my audience with a man from Spokan who had heard of us, and the paper sent him down to listen. I felt like I was pooping ice cycles as I entered the stage. The girls from town had me dressed in my finery and I was scared to death. I made an instant decision that I would split the music between the piano and my flute. My mother refused to help me. She said she just couldn't handle it now that the time was near. I was on my own. I went to the front of the stage and retold the story of how I got my Name. I lay the flute on top of the piano and began to sing and play. I would play a verse using the piano, and then switch to the flute. I did this a few times before finishing my song. I was failing at my attempts of doing this. And then little Nalin then entered the stage. She sat at the piano playing the chords; with a smile! she saved the day!!! My Mother was crying as I turned to the Audience. She started the clapping and I brought the house down. I went on with other songs that the damn drunk had taught me. Nalin and I had the crowd spellbound as the evening went on. Before leaving the building the news paper man interviewed me. I cut him short with my anger for Bill!!! I was ready to clobber him. I sent Nalin home and she was crying. I told her I have something to do!! She made me promise not to hurt him. I was glad she did this.

I was dressed as nice as any woman in town. It was late in the evening but the people were walking around. I "Ran" to the saloon and found him drunk on the boardwalk. I was screaming in his face telling him (&&(^%%%*% you damn drunk. I grabbed him by the collar and drug him back to the town hall. I demanded the Sheriff lock him up!! He said are you SURE!!! I said #%^*(*&^ you damn right I'm sure!! I left him there for a week.

After his week, he came to apologize to me! I let him have it again. He hung his head down and mumbled something. Nalin shook her finger at him and said shame on you Grandpa Bill. This made him Laugh. I told him I was trying to save enough money to put Mother in the hospital!! He looked at me strangely and said I have plenty of that!! I told him I haven't learned to count yet and I can't handle everything!!! He said he wouldn't promise me; but he would try it again. Nalin crawled to his lap and hugged him. She looked to his eyes and told him she "Loves him". I went to him and hugged him and told him that this is all that I ask. The growling bear was 'Back'!!! I never figured out how it happened. But that little Nalin took him by his hand. She would lead him through town past the "Evil Spirits" just a talking all the way. She became the most important part of our band. We were walking home swinging her between us just having fun. It was evening when we heard the sound of two buffalo guns. Nalin and Bill ran to the general store and I ran to the corner of the saloon. I saw them just sitting there mounted to their horses; they didn't run away this time. The sheriff came to us and said nobody was hit. I asked him if he would pursue them. He said he has tried this before, but they quickly are out of his jurisdiction when they ride. I told him next time this happens they will be at the end of my lance; that I would ride behind them to town. The sheriff just laughed. He told me the tale of the man they now call "buffalo stump" that came to him with a complaint!! He said thank God he don't know your name. He talked of him being a "Eunuch" and figured he wouldn't be much trouble no more!!! He said he told him he would look into this for him. He then spit on the ground and said he "looked". He asked me to let him do his job. The buffalo men then rode off. The Sheriff smiled and went to his office. My blood slowed down to a sizzle!!

Bill had a friend who worked for the papers of news. I really didn't know what this was. He told me he would ask for help with this using the "paper" to explain the problem. Little Nalin asked him to have the man meet us at the café where he could hear our music. Bill erupted with "That's a good idea!!!" He picked her up and held her in his arms; He told her she was "Smart"!! She was smiling in his face and told him; I know it Grandpa!!!! We were "cracking" up laughing.

We took Mother to the hospital and prepaid for her care. I demanded to talk to the doctors and nurses. They all knew of me, and the doctor had seen me dragging Bill down the street. I told them I wanted the best care they could give her, with no little remarks about the color of her skin. I told them she is "My Mother" and I wont put up with any hatred. The Doctor laughed and said he sewed up the hand of the buffalo hunter; and other areas that needed attention!!! he smiled and promised his respect. I think I got the message across!! They called her Miss Lozen!! And they kept her comfortable. I stopped by to visit her each day and she asked what the fuss was all about?? I told her she was being shown the respect that was due for her. She said it's just a baby!! I told her "NO" it's "Your Baby" and went to work. I was getting as good as her with my short quick answers.

I had the bar stock a keg of "Root Beer" for Bill and Nalin to drink. Bill drank till he floated. I got used to him using the out-house with frequent stops during the days. We were refining our music to fit in the piano with Misses Smith on the keys and Nalin helping her. Misses Smith would stretch out Nalin's fingers and tell her "stretch them"!! She did this as she played the chords. One day Misses Smith just looked at her; and told her she will have the hands of a frog some day!!! Bill still preferred his guitar to keep the music flowing. He moved little Nalin's chair to the piano bench next to him. He would stop the music and look to her face; and ask her to join him for a beer. "ROOT BEER"!! The owner complained, but Bill told him &%^%%^ and the music went on. My English had improved so much that I quit the school. We were working so much that I was getting tired. But I kept up the pace to keep Bill on his path.

Mother was about due with the Baby and Kenasher and the Chief were coming to town. The Chief didn't care about my music but he was there for Mother. I was talking to Kenasher when he finally could take no more. He demanded I call him "Ken-Asher" with the "look" on his face. After a long look I told him I'll work on it!! The &^&^%% fool. I went to get ready for work and put on the gown from Paris. Misses Smith did my hair up, and I really looked white. I was getting used to this and it was just normal anymore to me. But when Kenasher came to my dressing room it was like I knocked him to his knees. He just kept telling me I was "Beautiful" and followed me with his eyes. I tapped on his nose and told him "Patience" What a scamp I was!!! Misses Smith then dolled up Nalin!! She shined as bright as the sun. Her mother was crying as she entered the stage, with happiness she saw the beauty and the talent. With a swing of her fist she said "you get them little girl", Nalin would stand next to the piano and stretch out her arms with her fingers locked together, And you could hear them "Crack" to the back of the room!!! Misses Smith would then scold her for doing this!! Nalin would smile and say "OK!

When I came to the stage the people were clapping for me, I noticed my School Teacher talking with Bill. I excused myself for the moment and went to Bill to see what was going on. My Teacher then introduced me to "Glenda" whom she said played the best violin in the country. Bill said we could try her, by splitting up the music, He said he would finish his set, then my set, then we will let Glenda take it from there!! We started the music and when we turned it to Glenda; I was absolutely on my knees for this girl. She was looking at me as she took over with a smile on her face. I felt the whole room moving with the flow from her violin. She used her elbow to get me to join her with the flute!! And I will never, never, never forget the applause from the crowd. She was "Beautiful" The audience had three new people in it that were from the papers. And my trail was set. I got a telegraph message from the man that I met and he offered me a job there for more money then it was possible to think of. He said he would wire the money for the trip, and I was happy beyond belief.!!!

I was getting ready for work the next morning when the boom from the buffalo guns sounded. I just saw red blood running through my eyes, and ran to my horse with my lance in my hand; and jumped on his back. The Elder grabbed the reins and told me "NO" He asked that I let the sheriff handle it. I started crying and begged him to let me go!!! He said Nalin needs me now, to get off the horse. I got back down and apologized for my anger. I went to Nalin's lodge. Nalin and her Mother were sitting there crying. I gathered them close. There was nothing I could do. We said a prayer and the day moved on.

Mother gave birth to the most beautiful little girl in the world!!! As she handed her to me: She said: She was born on the seventh day, of the seventh month. By the "Seventh" wife of the Chief!!! And the Chief took his horses and left!!! I asked Kenasher if the chief wanted to see his baby?? He said he was making eyes at his horses!! We all laughed and life moved on. I now had another little sister to look out for and I would let Lozen hold her once in a while. I loved her more then the money in the bank. Bill was reminding me that we were due in San Francisco soon and that I had better deal with it. I could see it in his eyes that something was wrong. I sat with him and asked him of this. He was nearly crying when he told me of his love for the little Nalin, that her mother will never let her go. I asked him when he talked to her of this? He said he just got back from her home. Nalin then came running in and held him and they held each other crying. She told him I need You!!. She made him promise not to drink the spirits and to help me out with this. He finally said "ok" He told her "I will be back" and to finish with her schoolwork, and told her he "Loves her" She said she would wait. She said I love you forever and ever Grandpa. She had adopted him and he lived for her. I hugged her goodbye and left them alone.

This is where it started. Mother was having trouble walking. She was struggling with it and broke her hip. The doctor did what he could for her, but said she needed some different care that they only do back east. I went to Mother and talked with her of this and she said to worry about me first, and she will be okay. I told her she was supposed to try walking every day! She said, "Get out of here" I didn't want to argue and I went back to work. I was starting to feel the pressure of success.

I told Bill what had happened with Mother. He said that does it. He turned to Nalin and promised he would be back, that we needed the money for Mother first, He asked that she help her, and made her promise, she said she would do all that she can do. With tears in their eyes they said goodbye, I looked at Bill, I took a half a man with me that day. I asked Mother if I was right to leave her behind? She said she feels no evil around her! She then asked me of my dreams. I told her it's the same, I just see us watching the herd. She was playing her flute and stopped suddenly. She said she feels a quiet time. She smiled and just said; "GO"

We were booked at the Caledonian Club for a run of six months. Frisco was alive with the people of all colors and talents that made the city swell with pride!!! I had never in my life could have imagined what lay beyond the reservation. We were wined and dined at the best the town had to offer. I finally fell to the arms of Kenasher, and I rode him like a horse. Tee Hee!!! Yee-Haww. He was Hansom in his suit looking "Dapper" as he walked down the street. I almost forgot. We were married after that!!

Bill had taken Glenda under his wings. He taught her how to look for the talent that lays there waiting for a chance to do what it takes. He told her he didn't care if she was the best in the world; that it's not your violin that moves to the song!!! He taught her that it's an ear for the talent that matters, because that's how we make it a song!!! Glenda took a new look at the world. With our popularity starting to wane. She started listening to the other acts, to their voice, to their songs, to their talents. Bill said to imagine how you would fit in with them. This put a hunger in her heart for talent. She hung to each word he spoke as she went. I watched, as she became a warrior for music. For the fame, the fun, and the fans. She was like a locomotive with a half load of steam, near ready for her trip down the tracks.

I was fighting with everybody over my little sisters back home. I wanted to be a part of their life too. I could have no children for the same reason as mother. The doctors shut down her Baby machine and told her no more!!! I was still fairly young yet and busy beyond belief. I took my grief to the family now and said,, LOOK. I have been gone for a year. I love you all to death. But there is more to life then Music.

I told them they can dress me like the Queen of England, and parade me around the town. But I miss my buckskins, and I miss sitting on the ground. I miss talking with mother over the camp fire at night. I asked Glenda to keep up her work, that I would join her when I could. I am a simple Indian girl. who misses the forest, the river, and the land. I said most of all I miss my two sisters!!! I begged "please" let me do this??? Bill was in his usual mood. He told me "don't let the door hit ya in the butt when ya leave" He's so kind!! He instantly started with you don't need me no more!! I tore into him with $%&%^*&^&^ You old bastard, you promised me you will try, and were not done yet. I told him I feel it in Glenda, that she needs just a little more of your time. I praised him for all that he had done. I then reminded him of Mother!! I said she's the reason I'm here!! And she's not doing well, I asked about the money we needed for her care? He felt we had enough for the surgery. He was waiting to hear back from the therapy people. He made me cross my heart and hope to die before I left. Stupid old man!!! He made me promise to come back. I told him I promise. I asked him to work on the act, and teach Glenda all that you know. With a tear in his eye he asked me to give Nalin a hug and tell her that grandpa misses her. I felt the size of a midget. I was stingy!!

Kenasher and I jumped a train and traveled back to Spokan, and were exhausted when we arrived. I "RAN" to my little sister and hugged with all that I had. I promised her I would hold her for three days non-stop. Mother said you can't do that to your sister!! I said ya wanna bet!!! I asked mother about her English, that I wasn't expecting that. She told me it was the help that I hired who had done this for her. I hugged her and said I love you Mom!!! She finally grabbed me and said I love you too. She told me of meeting Ken's father. She asked that I "Honor" him. This I promised to do!!! They were still living at the boarding house when we arrived home. I contracted with Ziggler lumber to build us our own. This home was in Spokan. We had so much fun taking my sister fishing and hunting that we stole her from her mom. I asked her if she was ready to get her name assigned to her?? She was a smart little "Twerp" She said she had picked it, but her nasty old mom wont let her use it. I told her to honor her mother, that she gave you all that you have!! She said all but my name!!! She wanted to be little black bear.

I told her the legend of the Bear and the Coyote that I sing of in my songs. I told her of her birth under the sacred signs of the "Triple Sevens" I held up respect for the "FOX" in the story for the bravery and sense that he showed!! I told her of "Bill the Bear" and the troubles that he had. I told her I still have to watch over him because he listens to the coyote whenever he's around, and that is always!!! She was flipping her bobber in the river and said, "Fox"! She kept flipping it and said, "I will think about this" I was thinking. You could say "Thanks Sis" but, "NOOOO" "What a wretched little child"!!! But I Love her to death!!

I made a trip to see Nalin; she had grown like a weed. I told her of Glenda learning to take over Grandpa's job, and I would send her grandpa back to her as soon as I could. She cried but held her head high and wished me good luck. I asked her how she was doing on the Piano?? She told me of trying to save money for lessons, that misses smith had moved away. I told her when I get back I want to live in Spokane, that I would take her to lessons there. I saw her face light up with happiness. She asked me to tell Grandpa she loves him, that she sends him a blessing each day. I held her with Love and affection, and told her hang tight!! That he "Loves" you too!!!

I asked her of the buffalo guns? She said they still hear them, but no one has been shot this year. She told me of the Sheriff riding to the reservation to walk them to school. She said he carries an open warrant to do this. I told her to walk in his shadow and hang onto his hand. He is a "GOOD" man!!

We were getting pressed for time now. I had to get back to work before Bill the Bear took a drink. The old Goat!! Kenasher spoke with the builders who promised to have Mother in her home before winter. Ken talked with his Father and he promised to help. We had completely forgotten about furniture for the home and were dealing with that. The schedule was behind and Kenasher spoke with builders to have them deliver the furniture and set it up for Mother Lozen and Kumbah when the time comes. His father told him not to worry. He said he would watch over her. We had only ten acre for the home and a few horses. But it was more then mother Lozen ever thought we would ever have. She was so Loving and appreciative of everything. She got along with Kenasher better then me anymore. They brought tears to my eyes when they said goodbye to each other. Mother asked me of my dreams? I told her there is no change yet; the herd is larger though. We didn't understand this. Kens father eventually had mother and Kumbah moved into his house. He said they watched as the house was built. I think he was color blind too!!!

When we got back it was pandemonium in life. Glenda said this is normal to her!! I was picking up where I left off, and singing and playing twice a night. I was afraid I would be bald from pulling my hair out from schedules and song changes, it was nuts.

I didn't know it. But Kenasher presented me with a birthday present. I asked him what day I was born??? He said sometime between January and January, so happy birthday. We had a ball that night. We danced and dined. He bought me a flute from Sweden that was made of golden polished brass, and had a mouth- piece that came as an extra. I was afraid to take it from the case!!! I rode tall in the saddle that night Yee Haa!!!

Glenda's mother was lonely for her family and we put her on a train home. Glenda said she didn't care if she ever saw Colville again. We were moving so much now that we were booked in Sacramento for six weeks. I was busy keeping Glenda on track while the boys were trying to derail her. I guess I hadn't paid the attention to Bill the Bear. He missed Nalin more every day. He kept his word to me and never had another drink. But he was robbed after arriving in Sacramento and we were notified of his death. I was sick. Life moved on but it gnawed at my guts. I sent a wire to Nalin of his death. I hired a privet investigator to stay on their tail. The sheriff was so busy with cattle rustlers and the like that he never paid much attention to somebody that didn't run cattle. They eventually caught up to the three of them. Two were shot and killed in the process of capturing them. I went to court for the last one that stood trial for this, and, "of coarse" he didn't pull the trigger!! But when the judge gave me a moment to speak to the dirty rotten no good lousy son of a bitch bastard that I was in tears and screaming. I even spit at him and told him he was a pile of shit. I was pissed. He left a hole in my life and I still haven't forgiven him. I shouted Go to hell you bastard!!! And I told him of Bill's Grand Daughter that was left alone. That he was all she ever had. I handed the court a picture of the two of them to give to him; and said keep this to remind you for the rest of your life. The judge sentenced him to life in prison with no chance for parole. Damn, I was pissed I was working and choking on this.

I then wired the news to Nalin's mother. That they all paid for what they had done. She replied that Nalin hasn't eaten or talked since this happened. I was sick. I asked her to buy the Piano from the store. I will send what he asks for it to him right away. I begged her to do this for me. To have it moved to the center house on the reservation, where she can make the music that the kids wish to hear. I asked that she play with pride in her Grandfather. Tell her he looks down on her every day. She was crying I think while I waited for a response. She sent "We love you" And I cried the rest of the day.

We were now being moved up and down the coast, and the shows got smaller and smaller. Like all things new to people, it grows old. It hurt to do this, but I left Glenda on the coast. A short time later she was offered a job. She now lives in New York. She can play classic and contemporary, but she's a country girl at heart. Kenasher and I moved our butts back to Spokane when we finished our last tour.

After a week with mother and Fox I booked a stage to Colville. I paid for a horse and went to the reservation. As I was riding in near the center house, I could hear the piano just making noise. I went to the door and was looking at her, with her head in one hand and the other plunking at the keys I was sick. I went back to the horse and pulled out my brass flute and stood outside the door. I started to softly play the song of the Fox and the bear. I was nearly done with the first verse when the Piano joined in. When I stepped inside I quit playing it. She just held me and cried.

We went to her mothers lodging and I met her new baby brother. Her mother had found her happiness in a strong young warrior. We talked of many things till we got down to Nalin. Her mother asked that she tend to her brother. She knew this was coming with tears in her eyes. I asked to look after Nalin as gently as I could. I explained that I could use her help to tend to my Mother. And that I would see to it that she gets lessons on the Piano. She said I know that you Love her the way I do. She looked to my eyes and said she's afraid she will never come back. I saw her side of this issue. I told her of my struggling with the family over my Mother to return just to see her. I told her of being part of the band. I told her I give my heart to the Spirit that guides me, for the sake of my mother, my husband, and Nalin. She was the first sister I ever had. I asked her to think on this. And I will stay a few days. I told her I want to go fishing, and take Nalin with me. I wanted to talk to her about her Grandfather. I felt responsible for what happened to him. But that I cant change this. I only wish to help. She was crying again as she said she's a bag of bones now. She was thin but I said nothing of this, and asked again to think on this.

We went to the river for "Fishing" I just love it when I do this. Its quiet and it clears my head. We sat next to each other talking, and after a moment of quiet; she turned to me and asked if I was the warrior woman that's talked of in her tribe?? After a moment I asked what that she hears. She looked at the water and talked of the tales that are told, of the blond hair and blue eyes that she just ask for justice, and that she asked to be left alone. I told her I remember meeting her. I told her she had nobody but her Mother to grow up with; till she made a friend along the way. I told her this friend showed her how to put Love in her life, and I thank her for this every day. I told of the last time I saw her was in the white mans courtroom. I looked at her and told her this is where I let her walk away!! I told her not to dwell on what makes you bitter, to let go of it. It's like a legend. Just let her and him walk away!!! She said she misses her Grand Pa. I said let him walk away. She leaned to my shoulder and said goodbye to him. And let him "walk away".

I stayed at the lodge with Nalin for this night. I shared a bed with her as she cried. It was about six in the morning when I awoke; and was looking at her, with a smile on her sweet little face. I asked her what makes her happy??? She said she remembers me dragging Grandpa down the street!!! I started laughing and told her that was a moment that doesn't make me proud. She sat up still laughing and told me of the people who were clapping their hands as I drug him to the Sheriff, and of her Mother saying "You go get em girl" We were both cracking up as her Mother came in looking frightened!!! And she asked us what on earth is this about??? While my tears were running down my face I told her we were talking of a legend!! And Nalin said she peed her panties!!! I smacked her with a pillow. We just laughed and laughed and laughed. Her Mother said may the Great Spirit look over you two, and left the room. When we finally caught our breath I asked her if she were coming with me to Spokan to learn the piano?? She answered I don't think so!! She looked at me and said this is where it started for you, and she feels Grandpa's spirit here. She said she doesn't want to leave her mother to face this, and her little brother is new in her life. She said she would rather start here. I was so proud of her. I told her I will see if I can find someone to give her lessons on the piano, and made her promise to eat and learn to play. She looked at me and said I'm Hungry!!! And it was the start of a new day.

After a couple of days of searching, I found a woman from the East. She had an accent that was German and talked tuff like Grandpa Bill did, and I thought this is perfect. I introduced her to Nalin and she spurted out with a "Guten Morgen" and we were laughing again. She said "Dis always happen" I introduced her as Frau Mia, and they sat there talking. I said goodbye to her and her mother and I jumped on the stage. The three of them waved goodbye!! I felt pride in my heart for helping with this, so proud that I didn't even cry!!! In fact; I was laughing about dragging grandpa Bill down the road!!!!

I returned to my family in Spokan and the sun shined down us as I arrived. I just held them and loved them with all that I had, and waited for the bomb to drop, as I settled into life.

Kenasher' s father died. Ken was upset about this; and Ken took over his job. He made plenty of money to run the family and I got to watch my sister grow up. And no more Ken(&^^&$. She was seven now, and pretty as a picture. This is where it starts with school and all. Ken demanded she be sent to the white school. He said she needs a proper education. Mother was worried; she asked if this ever happens? Ken said if they want to collect the tax money from the mill and for our house!! It will happen. I sent Ken with her and said "Sick Em" she was accepted. Glad I wasn't there for that meeting. On her third day she got in trouble with a girl for fighting with her; and I went to meet with her teacher. I explained where and why that we came from, and told her that her mother usually speaks the Sahaptian language. She told me she's like a bomb, ready to explode. It took me back to the "Good old days" tee hee. I asked her what she wanted me to do?? She was thinking, she asked how miss Lozen kept me under control when I was young? I was laughing, I told her she didn't leave me an inch that living in the middle of nowhere and feeding us was a full time job since I learned how to walk. I was thinking. I told her we did have our quiet times, and she taught me to play the flute. I told her the Lozen has been ill every since she gave birth to her, and that I promised her that I would never, never, never take her away from her. I told her of the doctor that watches over her, but he has done all he can do. She told me that back East they have "specialist' doctors and she would help me with that. She asked many questions about mother, and I told her she holds her close. She said that's what I thought, she said she never saw her on the streets in town, and her mother cant walk or don't want to. I said your telling me, that she needs friends? She said, "You hit the nail on the head"!!! I asked her if all the girls avoid her because of her red skin. She said most!! But not all. She told me of the two Johnson girls that tried to play with her, but that she puffs herself up on the defense and they gave up. I told her mother has always been that way. She asked that I figure out a way to take them both and learn to mingle. I was laughing and told her it will be the three of us to learn this, that I was never good at it either. She said I should work on her wardrobe too. She leaned back in her chair and said; "Good luck".

I went first to Mother Lozen and told her of the problems. I told her it starts with her "Name" that not to many girls are called "Fox" and the way that we send her to school in her buckskins. And her "Attitude" I took the blame for her name. She picked up her flute and started playing a soft tune. She stopped and looked at me, and said her "NAME". I just shook my head up and down. She finished her tune and told me to work on her name, and she will work on her buckskins. I asked about her attitude. She said "she" will have to work on that. I was just looking at mother. I had an idea and ran it past her. I asked her if I should go to her school and tell the tale of the fox and the bear to the kids. I felt that if I told the story they would understand why she proud of her name. She told me I was wise.

I had learned a bit of introducing the music and I was comfortable with this. The teacher and I made it a history lesson for the kids, and it was starting to be "Fun" I borrowed a pair of buckskins from mother and told her she's coming with me and to bring her flute. She said, "^%#$#$" I said your welcome!!! The teacher gave us the whole day to do this; I set up the classroom with the Indian treasures from our travels. I set up mom and her flute to the side of the teacher's desk. I had Kumbah make fry bread and porridge and we had a ton of fun with this. We pushed the kids desks to the side and spread blankets on the floor. We had feathers and beads for the children and we were ready.

Mother was playing the flute as the kids arrived. Fox was at the door to greet them. She gave feathers to the girls, and gave arrowheads to the boys, and seated all of them. Mother was smiling now and she put down her flute. I thanked them for coming, and started the story. Mother started softly playing the song. When I told of the fight with the fox Mom gave it all that she had!!! Then I soften the tale and mother, soften the flute, and we drifted them down the river. Those kids were in awe of her after doing this. And asking for a new name for themselves!!! We fed them lunch and they asked many questions. Mother handled it with great pride. She had Fox next to her to translate the questions. And the kids now understood. It opened a door with her classmates. This would follow her till she was done.

As time went by, Lozen had her in a riding skirt, which looks like a dress with puffy pant legs. Ken came home from work one night and told me I was doing this all wrong. He said if you put a dress on a pig it still oinks and you will never, never, never, change that. He asked me if I have ever noticed that she's closer to the horses then any person that walks this earth?? I said their just horses. He went to Lozen and asked her if he could help. She said he could do more for her than I could. I said)&&^^(and left the room. Ken got her involved in barrel racing and she had fun with that. He asked me to pick another Indian girl who likes horses, and he would buy her a horse if she really puts her heart into it with the race. I did some checking with the school, there was a half-breed girl that was a year ahead of her in school. She had the same problems as Fox did, but I was told she was quiet. Her name was "Ann", she was named Ann by her late father. They lived at the edge of town in a run down cabin. Her mother spoke "Sahap-lish" which is half and half. I talked with her and she was scared of what I was trying to do. I brought my mother with me to talk to her and she smiled as big as the sun. Mother Lozen "Dispatched" Ken to the ranch and fixed up the barn, and bought her an Appaloosa Mare. I took her to town with me and bought her some dresses and had her hair fixed to where she fit in. Ken taught her of riding and gave her all the time he could. By the end of the school year she was ready. We had to make her an example to follow, and she was as sweet as an apple; and followed Ken with Love. I felt terrible and went to Mother Lozen crying and told her I never learned how to handle this. She said "times are changing" I told her I went from the bottom to the top overnight and never lived in between like she does. She said teach her what you know, and let Ken do the rest. That she "Trusts" him with his patience. I told her that she gets along fine with her classmates now. I said I wish we had done this for the whole school. She picked up her flute and looked at me. And said "The whole school"

Oh boy; we were on a roll now. We bought tubs to cook the fry bread and set up spits to cook the beef. The weather was nice so we held it outside. Ken had billings printed and he called it "Motto Teep Alo. Which is (home of the bear) Fox's teacher helped out with everything? She talked with all the people in town. We invited the local tribe to join us, and they mixed in with the crowd. The tribe brought their drums and the people just listen, and they all had fun. I had mother and the tavern band with me. We told the story four times this day. Mother was wise. She told me that it takes more then the kids to change people's attitude toward the tribes. We made friends with a lot of them this day.

We had it started now and I turned my attention to mother Lozen. I had found a doctor that was a specialist in Orthopedics. He was back East but he was a young and inventive kind of doctor that helped a man here in town who was really suffering to work, and he works every day now. We were lucky just to have a doctor!! It wasn't easy, but I kept after Mother till she gave in and agreed to try. I think when she saw Ken working with Fox, she was happy. Though she did her best to raise her, she would have kicked my butt to death for doing what she shouldn't do!! I went to Ken and told him I was going to take Mother back east for her treatment. He said I should have done it five years ago!! I smacked him a good one for that comment!! But he's right.

I looked at what we were doing now and realized that we were in transition, that my mother was getting older and it was time to take the horse by the reins and steer it down the trail!!!

I was packing my cloths and I had the flute that Ken had bought for me in the drawer. I still liked my old wooden flute but decided to take the new one with me. I took it from the case and was playing it, and I realized it was capable of the high notes much better then the wood was. I finally had time to do what I wanted to do. I had Ken buy the tickets to New York and asked him of money. He said he would send me what they and I need, to find a bank back there, that I would be there for a while. I hadn't thought that far ahead of myself. I took a deep breath and kept on moving.

I got in touch with Glenda because she lives there now. Her career was solid and she would stay there and have privet bookings and a few appearances at the music halls. She said she was just getting tired of keeping up to it. I laughed and told her "I know what you mean." Glenda offered me a room in her house to stay with her while mother goes through this. She said she was within a mile of the hospital and I took her up on her offer. Glenda now worked for a company in California part time as a talent scout.

Mother still had a muscular structure to her body. She would struggle with it, but the pain was unbearable for her to keep on going. She hated the wheelchair and cursed it till it was afraid of her!! Yikes!! I went through pure "Hell" to get her there, there were so many stops and switching trains and it wasn't easy. When we arrived we were both taken with the city. It was "Modern" and the way of life was much different in the East. People there were much more color blind, and they offered their help with mother and I to get us through the train station. When we reached the station in New York it was the same. The conductor called out for a man to push the chair for me, and the people were fascinated with mother because she was a true Indian Woman, and they showed her respect. She had picked up a bit of the English after raising Fox, and she needed it now. I was still nervous about it but mother was fine. We found Glenda and she steered us down the path. We were just about to her apartment when mother said she should have bought a dress. I was without words for that one!! The kids were the ones that impressed mother. They would have sat there all day to speak with her, but when she took out her flute, She had them captured. Mother was older now but her steel gray eyes light up with Glee when the kids come a running.

New York is home to the Seneca Tribes. I asked Glenda to help me contact their Elders so I could keep mother busy. She told me of them living among the whites, she said they see no difference, that they dress like we do, they speak pure English. She said unless they have a Pow Wow they just live among us. It was so busy there that I couldn't believe it. She showed me their reservation and left it up to me from there. I spoke with the elders that were there till I found the one most like Mother. I told him of why I was here, and he offered his help with this. He was a schoolteacher and the kids were on a summer break. I was so appreciative to him. He was a man of few words. Like mother. He was a warrior at heart. And he understood my feelings too. When I introduced him to mother!!! It was like the Great Spirit pulled back the clouds. He went to her side and talked with her softly!! And mothers heart melted right there in my site!! I had never seen this before. Her heart melted in his hands. The language was much different here and he spent the first day just figuring out "How" to talk with her. But they were making progress. Whenever he would smile: I could hear her heart beat rising, Like a volcano ready to blow!!! She had always told me that her heart tells her to move west. But I saw the Golden leaf of the maple tree blow her leaf to the East. Her steel gray eyes never left him. Not for a minute since they met. For as far as I can remember: They were just Indians, including the Chief of the tribe that her daughter comes from. I couldn't believe it!! She shown with her beauty, for the man she has found.

We got Mother into the doctor and he did his exam. He did test after test on her and asked her to stay at the hospital while he works on this, that she was having pain from an old injury and it's not easy to fix this. I asked how much time he needed. He was looking at mother with his hand on his mouth thinking. He turned to me and said maybe as much as a year with therapy. I wasn't prepared for this. I asked him when do you want to start?? He said, "we might as well start now, she's here"!! I went to Mother and her friend "Achak" and told them of what the doctor said. Mother started to protest this and Achak put his hand on her shoulder and she calmed down. He said the days of the medicine man are gone now, to listen to the words of the white doctor if you want to walk again. She took a long look in his eyes, and I could see that she had trust in him. She said she would do this; she then said, they better like flute music!! I was laughing as I got her to her room. Her friend sat with her and told me to go. I was insulted!! But I went.

Glenda had a concert to go to and invited me along. I had nothing else to do and I went. I just do what I'm told to do!!! ^(&&((Y#^$#$%&$^%. We arrived at the hall and it was beautiful. It had curtains that rose to the sky, and wood- work that was perfect. She had me seated in the front with the people of great stature. She came on stage and she was wild, as she would strike the strings at the speed of light and she got applause that was like thunder.

I wasn't prepared for this. She stopped and brought up our career together when she started, and pointed right at me, I stood and took my bows and was ready to sit back down. She had a man bring my flutes to the stage!! I thought, you little thief!!! I had more fun that night as we played the "old tunes", with the audience just going "Crazy" I stayed on stage with her to the end of the show. She stood on stage and told the people of my mother. When they heard this they sent me a feeling of compassion for me. She had me do the story of the Bear and the Coyote for her last number. I used my old wood flute for this. I thought the roof would fall in. with the violin she brought it out to perfection. She then promised the people to have The Lozen appear when she's ready!!

After leaving the stage, I was offered a contract. Glenda made me contact Ken the next day. I was a working girl again. I was so happy, I thought that part of my life was gone, but a new place, new people, this will end too. I never got the chance to ask about Fox. The telegraph can only ask a question, and wait for an answer. And it was busy. I went to talk with Mother Lozen and told her of what happened. She was happy for me I think?? She was totally taken with "Achak" I saw her eyes light up like a candle. I tried to talk with her but Achak told me I better go, he didn't want her to get over excited.!!! After thinking about it. I have never seen her so excited, and it's not about me!!! Mother asked about Fox?? I told her I was sorry but the telegraph was busy!! She got a "serious" look on her face and asked me; "how do you talk through the wires"??? I thought about my response to her question. I told her of the man who taps on the wires and uses a code like sending smoke signals!!! She asked; how does he see them??? I didn't know what to say. I didn't understand completely how this worked myself. I told her the man has the eyes of an owl and he uses them with his wisdom. I said he sends the message to his father who is the watcher who looks over the forest with his eyes. I told her of the brother of the owl who reads the message and repeats it like a war chant!!! Achak left the room laughing so hard that he nearly smothered to hide it. Mother picked up her flute. She said the "Owl" And played the song of the owl!!! I went home and told Glenda what happened. She was standing there rolling her eyes in a circle looking "Coo Coo". I whacked her and laughed myself. She gave me a long silent look. Then said lets do this. We picked up our gear and started. It was different from the way we had done this before. She put more of herself into it. She asked me to just copy her movement and tunes. We had a week to get ready.

The next day the costume people came and measured and fussed over us. I let Glenda pick what we should wear; I was more into the music then the cloths. She was done and shooed them off and came to see how I was doing. I showed her where I wanted to use the wood and the brass, and had only two songs where I would sing. She was looking at this and decided to add a singer in the mix. She had met a young women that auditioned for her and thought she would fit her in. This is when I met Kathy. With one phone call she was there. It made me jealous to call her because we didn't have them in Spokane yet. She had a beautiful voice. She could match the high pitch of the brass flute. Glenda would join us once in awhile but I mostly worked with Kathy. She amazed me. Glenda ran the whole show; on her own. Times have changed. Kathy stayed with us here at Glenda's and we worked very hard on our show. We had one day to go when Glenda out of nowhere shut us down and demanded we go see Lozen. I thought the stingy little thing would never get around to that!!

We went to her room and I brought her up to date on her Fox. Achak was now holding her hand. She had her eye's start to water and

Achak kicked us out of there. When we were in the hall, Glenda started rolling her eyes. Kathy was laughing so hard I thought she would pee her panties, she told her she looks GOFFY when she does that!! So she did it again and we both were laughing. She said "Shes Happy" and we giggled our way home. I was really starting to enjoy this. Glenda and Kathy were talking about the costumes, and she wanted three changes per act. We were to start with "Beautiful and end wearing buckskins. I asked why not buckskins for the whole thing, Tee Hee!! And she bonked me on my head!!! It was just plain fun. I tried to roll my eyes around like Glenda does; But Kathy said, "Give it up"

There were advertisements hung all over the city for our show. The theater put all they had into this. When we peeked from the curtains it was a packed house. We were standing there holding hands and Glenda said a prayer over us and we went to the stage. The show was a hit, and Glenda's idea of having Kathy read the legend of the Bear and the Coyote worked perfectly as I played the wood flute for its entirety. We had three Encores this night, and the word was around the town already. It had twice the impact that I remembered from our start of this.

We were settling down now and went out for dinners. This was where I was introduced to "Comedy" I couldn't understand the menu and just had the same as what Glenda had ordered and we kept working on our act. When they brought us our dinner it came in "Courses" and they sat a bowl of noodles down for each of us. I couldn't get them to stay on my fork and was complaining about this!!! The crazy women Kathy just picked up her bowl and dumped them on her face!!! She was chewing on what she got in her mouth and looking at me!!! I was losing it, I laughed till I peed my panties. The waiter came a running, apologizing for the mess!!! She turned to him and growled like a wolf and scared him away too!! Glenda just looked at Kathy and said we wont eat here again. I laughed for two days.

The three of us went to tell Mother Lozen the next day. We were all excited as we entered her room. Achak asked us to settle down. I mumbled $%&^^%$&#. I told her of the concert and of the applause and the encores. She patted my hand and told me this is good and turned back to Achak. I asked mother if she wanted me to ask anything

of Fox over the telegraph?? Achak ran from her room laughing!!!—
Glenda then started rolling her goofy eyes---I had to leave the room.-
--When were working' Shes all work. When she playing goofy eyes,--
She's Nutts!!!! She made me wonder if I would have ever made it home
if I had turned it over to her when we started. I asked her on the way
home if we were going to keep the wardrobe of dress, blue jeans, and
Indian gear going. She said I don't know, she asked what I thought of
the Indian gear?? I laughed and told her of wearing little chickadee
feathers, that this is a first to wear a peacock feather strait up like a
mans. She said ill work on that!!

After our third show Mother Lozen was ready for surgery. As they
were rolling her away I told her how much I loved her. She answered
with a smile. She made me feel positive about this. The four of us held
hands and said a prayer for her. Then came the waiting.

Achak was so worried he just paced the floor. Mother was thin
like us girls, and I never figured out what he saw in her. I got up and
went to him. I was looking into his worried eyes. I asked him straight
out, "What do you see in her". He told me he knew she was the one
from the first time she held his hand. With his eyes lit up he told
me how after talking to her it was even more. He told me she was
Beautiful inside and out. He nearly had tears in his eyes when he said,
"She just has to get better." I asked him if she ever talked of me?? He
said I know you now. That I saved her from a life of blood. He told me
there are no "words" to describe her love for you. I told him it's not
clear to me why she saved me. I told him I still need her in my life. I
told him of my Love for her, that she is my Mother. He said I know, he
apologized for running me off the other day. I told him he was "Stingy"
He finally laughed. He said yes I am. He told me of waiting for marriage
to a woman from his tribe. He said he never found her. Till he met my
mother. I asked him what she said of the little Fox. He smiled and told
me of her love for her too. I sat back in my chair and told him I felt her
love. But that she never showed it to me the way she does for you. He
told me that he felt she was scared that the white man would take you
from her!! I told him I will be in my grave before that will happen. He
took me into his arms and we sat quietly. I fell asleep.

Achak shook me awake, they were bringing mother out of surgery. She had been in there for hours. The surgeon was trying to explain what the problem was, but none of us understood what he was talking about. I stopped him and asked him, "Will she be better!!" He chuckled at himself, and said she will be fine! He then talked of "Therapy" for her.

We all were so relieved to hear the news. We were taken to her room where she was awake but she looked like she had just come back from fighting with the bear. We all showed her our love for her and they asked us to leave. I sent the girls home and sat with Achak and he came out of his grief. He was a friendly man now. It was like somebody had lifted the weight of the world from his chest. He talked to me non-stop for the next six hours. The nurse came to us and asked us to see her one at a time. Achak smiled and told me to go first!! This made me happy to see his stingy heart melt.

I was holding her hand so tight that she asked that I stop this. We talked and talked. I finally had to turn her over to Achak, and she smiled!!! I asked her if she had found the Love that she searched for?? She smiled and said "NO" He found me!!! I left the room laughing. Achak ran through the door to Mother, and I was thankful to God for him and my mother. I ran to send a message to Ken and the Fox. Ken said the Fox has still not forgiven me yet for making her stay home. I messaged back---boo hoo.

We kept going with the shows, as Mother grew stronger. I stopped by each morning to visit and they were walking her around now. I saw the smile on her face return to her and she was gaining her strength. She was amazed at the people who worked with her as time went on. She told me she thought everybody hated the Indians. I laughed and told her that the east has robbed them of all that they could, and now their just "Brothers." She looked around, and said she thought I was right. Achak stayed right there with her as they moved her to a different hospital for her therapy. She was gaining her strength back in her body and soul. Her steel gray eyes; showed with fire in them. She told me she had waited for this for a long time. That she felt love in her heart for Achak and she missed the fox. I told her school will be out soon and Ken will bring her here to see you. She said "Really" I laughed and told her that the Fox leaves him no choice. Mother was picking up the English language quickly. I think it was from being desperate to talk with Achak. I told her if you can't beat them, "Join them" I walked her through the "Maze" as I called it. She was getting stronger and stronger. Achak was a teacher at the school there in town and had returned to work. He shared a bed with her now and he did all he could do for her. I asked her the question that I dreaded. I asked her if she was coming home or does she want to live in the East?? She said Achak isn't sure about moving west. That he wants time to think about it. I said that's fine, that I will not force him to answer this. She was able to stand on her own now, and I invited her to the theater!! She said I think I'm ready with an amazed look on her face.

The group at the theater set up a special performance venue for mother to appear. We had a following of fans for our music now that they were excited to meet her. I told mother she was the "Key" to our band of girls; it all started with her. I explained how I told the story of our life and what we had been through. She looked at me with a long look, and said "I make her proud".

We had the wardrobe people come to mother to fit her into her costume. She said she just never seen so much fussing. I was laughing at her and told her it gets worse when you appear every night!! The people that worked for the theater were used to me now. I had them tie the chickadee feathers to her hair and they "Fluffed and Buffed" her to perfection. She was a beautiful Lady to say the least. She couldn't stop looking at herself in the mirror. Achak was ready to pass out when he looked at her, and told her she was "Georges" She asked what is Georges?? He said "Absolutely Beautiful". She turned back to the mirror and said thank you to him. She was a "Looker I'll tell you" She walked across the room with no help from anyone and gave him a kiss.

I had not mentioned it to Mother yet, but Ken and the Fox would be there to see her performance. I had been practicing with her and she was ready for this. I picked them up at the station and hid them from her. I sneaked Achak in to meet Fox and Ken and they were impressed with him. She was still in the care of the hospital and she and Achak were still there. The theater sent a coach to bring her to the theater, and she walked to the building with our fans just raising a fuss. I was surprised that this didn't scare her.

The theater had a whole orchestra set up in front of us, and a master of ceremony announced us as we stood there waiting. I gave mother a kiss and asked her to think of our time in the forest, and Ignore, the rest of this. The girls and I did our numbers and the master came on stage to announce mother. It was like sitting in a thunderstorm as she walked out on stage. We had two chairs which mother and I sat in. the two girls were behind us as the show began. With Kathy softly singing Mother played the old tune. With her eyes shut she drifted us through time, with her song of the Bear and the Coyote. When she was done, she stood as the audience went crazy, and it rolled on with thunder. I finally, saw a long honest smile on her face as she looked to the people. It was a smile that will never leave her face again. Mother stayed there with us till the end of the show. She played it in unison with me as we had done so long ago. My pride in her was so great that I started to cry; with a smile she brought me back to this earth. She stood again for the end. She then saw her family in front of her. The Fox could take this no longer and ran to her on stage. While she was holding her Glenda called the whole family to the stage, and we held each other with a happiness sent from God. You could hear the cheering for blocks from the people outside. The house was packed and the street was too.

Mother was bristling with her strength by the end of that summer. She would appear with us on Saturdays, and she was introduced to shopping in town, she and Achak would walk the town shopping and this was part of her therapy. She was recognized now as the Great Mother of the West. Like Sacagawea she had gained her fame. I had to show her how to spell and sign her name, and I did this with such pride that I felt her love pouring over me as she was asked to sign the peoples programs. She said she never could have imagined that it would have ever turned out like this. I just cried and held her.

Ken finally told me of Ann's mother. He said he had moved her to the house after Ann refused to go home to her. Ken told me of her way of living that he called "traditional." He told me of Ann crying herself to sleep at night. He said it made it hard for her to go to school, that her mother never agreed to that. He said he took an interpreter with him to her cabin and explained to her Ann's new life with the whites!

He said she never joins them for dinner. That she had a chair out on the deck and she slept there most of the time. He said that it made him close to Ann since the beginning of this. He laughed and called her his daughter. I told him I would council with mother when were home. He said I pray you have the answer.

The summer was a growing experience for little Fox. She also felt the love that passed between the people. She was tight to her mother and Achak and she just couldn't believe the respect shown for all of them. She told me one evening that she would look at those with "Pity" when she hears the comments in the west. Like the Great Chief Joseph, she said she will fight no more. I asked her if she missed the West?? She got a look on her face like her panties were too tight. She said she misses her "Horse." That's my sister!!!

Glenda said she was going to play this to the end. She hired two ladies to take our place that played the flutes and dressed them up like Indians. I thought oh wow, Shes a businessperson!! We boarded the train after an emotional goodbye. I was just glad we were done with this. We had first class tickets and we dined in the dinning car. Mother Lozen was after the Fox to get her face out of the windows. Fox looked at her and said MOM, were going so fast that I don't want to miss this!! Mother picked up her flute and played a short tune. Then looked at the Fox and said. With your Butt in my face I cant see it either. Fox said sorry mom, and moved down to the next widow. Tee Hee!! The little Fox had learned a lot on this trip. She was wearing a dress with pride. She enjoyed the attention paid to her in New York, and made Mother proud to call her Daughter.

We stopped for three days in Denver where Kens Grand Father lives. He was a rancher there of renown. We visited with he and his wife, and they told us the tales of old. They were of an age of transition and we all realized this. We looked at life differently as we grew. Grandpa was watching Fox play with his dog, and said he remembers the days that she would have been crying to do this, because of the fighting with them left their Souls empty of play. He was smiling when he said "Thank God" for this journey, that he has now seen it. He asked that we all remember this; that their Sacred Spirit never is looked at with blind eyes again. I nearly cried. We had a great seven days visiting.

Mother taught Achak to fish with nets and they had fun too. We said our goodbyes and were back on the train for our final ride home. Fox was exploding to tell her sister Ann of all she had met with and all that she learned of. She took her place at the window and we went flying down the tracks, and we were "Happy"

Ann brought the wagon to town to pick us up. We had a train full of luggage and goodies. Mother was shaking her head and told Ken that he should add onto the house before we take it home. He said she was right!!! The Fox had bought dresses for Ann and was trying to show her what she had bought. Ann just shook her head and ran to Mother and held her in her arms. She was so happy to see her walk again that she didn't care if Fox had bought her a train full of Gold. We were ready to go home now. I was looking for Mother. Achak nodded to our left and said she would be here when she is ready!!! I saw her talking to a young man. He was holding her tight. Turned out to be the boy that she saved on our trip to Oregon. He works for the railroad now, and had grown with the mussel of a bear.

Mother started to tell me in English! She then switched to Shahaptain. She told of a fight that was started by Honyauk over the boy's care that wound up over his being shot by Atsa. Seems Hanyauk mistreated the boy. And Atsa wouldn't stand for this. I told Mother I don't understand how he could be so kind to me and feel hate for the white boy. She said his name is "Glen" I never knew this before!! She told me of Atsa bringing him here to work for the railroad. She said he's fighting his hands but that he gets by and is happy just to be alive. I asked her of Atsa? She just shook her head. She had nothing else to say of this. I respected her privacy.

I spent the first two days never more then a footstep from the bed and the coffee pot. I was "Pooped" Fox was still attacking Ann with her goodies and she was making her wear a dress. Ann was starting to get mad at her and marched into my room and told me, "It just aint natural" She was a pretty little thing. I told her it's a new school year and she must learn to use her Beauty to her advantage. She said her horse don't care how she looks!! I laughed and told her probably not, but the boys in this town do!!! She left in a huff. Fox was listening to this go on and took her for a ride to town. She came back with a different opinion of what I had told her, and asked Fox to add the chickadee feathers to her hair. Fox gladly did this for her. Fox came to me later that night and told me that Billy Swenson whistled at her!!! We giggled and she ran like the wind.

Ken was busy at the mill filling the orders. Spokane was growing like a weed. I had taken over Ann's care and was watching over both Fox and Ann. Mother and Achak were busy with fishing and hunting, and a lot of loving too!!! He was the best thing that ever happened to her. Fox was now calling him "Father" and showed him her respect. They would sit together in the evenings and Fox would show them her homework from the school, and they would talk to her of how well she was doing.

I asked Mother Lozen for a council this night. I explained the problem with Ann's mother. She was playing her flute not saying anything. She finished her song and looked at me and said there's nothing that I can do to change her. She then laughed at herself and told me of her feelings when I first went on the road with my music. She said she nearly turned her life to what Ann's mother is going thru. She then chuckled and told me that as she sat in her wheel chair waiting to hear from me, that she thought life would never change. She called herself "Lucky" She then thanked Ken and I for helping her through the time of quietness. She said she couldn't believe her life turned out to be one of "Love" She asked that I make her life "Comfortable". She commanded that we all just give her the love that she needs. She asked that we not force her to do anything. Mother then picked up her flute and played it. When done she smiled at me and asked if this was all?? I told her I would add a blanket to her. She asked that I tell her "Goodnight"

Ann had taken to me now. She would sit with me and talk. She was a quiet little thing and she would pick up the old wooden flute and I taught her to play. Her mother was ill most of the time. She missed the "Old Ways" of living and never could get used to living in the house. She had a very long pipe and she would sit on the deck puffing on it and sing a song of the lonely coyote most nights. She passed her Soul to the "Spirit" who called to her. And she lay sleeping with a smile on her face. Ann was crying for her. I promised her that she was happy now. I gave her my wood flute after her service and she played it over her grave. It brought tears to my eyes to see this, and I held her tight to my side. I told her the story of Ayiana and of all she had done while gone from her tribe. I told her the story of my life, And of how I lost my parents to the Nations, and of my success in the world of music. I told her it all happens for a reason. I asked her to not look back with anything but Love in her heart. To let the Great Spirit guide her. And that I will always be there for you. Fox called her Sister, and asked her to join the family. I asked if she wanted to be adopted. I told her she could be the daughter of Xa'xats and Ken; that I feel it is what your mother wanted too. She held me tight and thanked me for this!! I told her to stop this. That the Spirit has spoken and life moves on for us as a family, and demanded she smile. She said I love you mother. Thru my tears I said I "Love you too"

I always felt inferior to the tribes when I was young. I had to battle my way to recognition. So I know what she's going through in life. With a sister she has someone to confide in. I just pray she trusts me as her mother. She was closest to Ken. She proudly called him father. She told me of everything he had done for her while I was gone to New York. But the one problem in her life that she faces, and leaves her outside and lonely. Shes a Half-Breed. That term alone is a nasty thing to say. So she gets this rubbed in her face by both sides of the kids in school. I think that's why she's so quiet. Shes afraid to say anything. I keep running this through my mind looking for an answer. I pray about it too, Its like there is an answer waiting for her and I vow to help her find it.

I started with the flute. Mother had taught me everything I know with this. But it takes a spiritual feeling to play one. She never had the feelings to put into it. After about two months I went to my Mother and talked to her. I knelt in front of her and looked to her eyes. I told her of my fear for Ann. I asked her how she would handle this. She looked at me and picked up her flute and played a soft tune. She was ready to start again and I saw it in her eyes that she realized something. She asked me about her singing the songs. She said she watched her shoeing the horse, and of how she kept the horse calm with her voice. She started playing it again. When she was done. She looked into my Soul and asked if I thought I could do this for her. I told her I will try, but I have no experience with this!! She finished the tune. She looked at me and said I have the connection with her. She talked of Ken with respect for him. She said he gave her feet. Her feet walked to you. She said be vigilant!! That the Great Spirit has given all of us a talent for something in our life. She said for some it's simple, that their happy just to breath. For some it's a tangled mess that she has to be unwound from the nets around her to find an answer. I lay my head in her lap, as she started playing it again. I felt about five years old living in the forest as the song went along. I was still laying there when she finished. I told her all I know is music. She was brushing my hair with her hand. She said she has seen the light in my eyes from the first note from the flute. She tipped my head to her, and said its more then the flute though. She said she watched me handle Bill; and the determination to bring it all together. I told her of my anger for the man who took his life. She told me like Ann losing her Mother, Bill was the one you lost. She said it made me stronger. I stood and thanked her for her counsel. I asked her if she would help me with this?? She said she was happy now that she had found Achak. She said she wants to live the rest of her life with him at her side. She told me she looked for what she now has for the course of her life. She said it's up to me now, that she will counsel me when needed. But I must travel this road by myself. I was so grateful to have her listen to me that I held her tight as I could, and told her "I Love You" She smiled over me and told me the same.

As time moved along I saw Ann get more respect for her because she dressed in a dress and carried her head high. But it wasn't enough to stop the comments from the men in town, and some of the women would stop and whisper as she walked by them. My heart told me to clobber them! But I knew this would make it worse.

Glenda called me on the new telephone system. We were having fun talking, and about a year had gone by since I was there. She told me of what she had been through to keep the show going, that once I left she never found the one to replace me. She had never met Ann, but I mentioned that Ken and I were in the process of adopting her. She then told me that she had booked a show with a six - month contract in Chicago, and she would have to put it together again when she gets there. We went on talking and she asked when Ann was out of school for the summer? I told her the first of June, which was close now. She asked me to bring Ann with me and come to Chicago; so she could meet with her; she said she's family now and she probably don't know how lucky she is. I told her I don't know what her talent is, that I have been looking and haven't seen it. She laughed and said bring her to me, Ill find it!!

I made a quick stop to telegraph the sheriff in Colville. He said nothing has changed. I sent my Love to Nalin and told her I was busy, that I would be there as soon as I could. I was so busy, I felt guilty for leaving her behind. I asked if the sheriff had gotten permission for tribel police? He said it starts next month. I thanked him. He said to say thank you to. Achak; that he had gone to the Stevens county council and demanded police for their protection. The sheriff was so busy anymore that he couldn't take time to cover them. He drew them to the center so they could control the borders with the police. This kept them far enough away to avoid being shot at.

I went and talked to Ken after this, He hated the thought of Ann being gone for the summer, but agreed to do this for me. I went next to mother and told her of this. She hugged me and told me I was wise. Achak said he loves her too, that he tried to help her but she is persecuted from both sides. I had tried everything I knew, and we boarded the train to the East.

Glenda picked us up at the station. She gave me a quick hug and turned instantly to Ann. She looked her in the eyes and started to walk around her looking at every detail she could. Ann was getting nervous, and Glenda was back in front of her now holding her chin in her hand. She asked Ann to speak!! She was just looking at her. Ann asked her about what? She asked if she knew any poetry? Ann thought for a moment and said she knew a little that she had done in school. Glenda said lets hear it!!! She very quietly quoted the words of Emily Dickinson in a nervous kind of voice. I saw Glenda's head going up and down as she shouted lets get loaded and get the hell out of here!! That's my Glenda!!

On the way to our rooms she told me of the new way of telling a tale before the music was introduced. She said most of the time it's a man who yells at the top of his lungs about nothing, and the orchestra saves him. She said she had been giving auditions for three days now and hadn't found what she's looking for. She said a soft voice that can speak and sing, and carries the feelings is what she's looking for, and she thinks she can train somebody better that has no experience with this, she said I don't like this, she said it just gets in her way. I was "IMPRESSED". Suddenly Ann said she can't talk in front of all the people; that she stumbled on her book reports that she read at the school. Glenda said those are teachers that don't know what they're doing, that she will train her if she has what it takes!!

We had dinner in a nice restraunt the first night, and Glenda kept telling her to relax. Ann said she gets the "Jitters" when she does this. Glenda told her to concentrate on her breathing and ignore the noise. She demonstrated to her what she asked of her and she settled down a bit. She told her to block out everything including your mother and I and just keep concentrating on breathing. Man; She had a way about her. She brought her back to earth. We had a good dinner and returned to our rooms. We visited for a time and Glenda got up to go. She was looking at Ann and went to the night table and pulled a Bible from it and asked her to start at Exodus and practice reading it. Ann was holding the Bible with a look on her face that would stop a freight train. Glenda said start now. She was reading it when Glenda told her to look at the light bulb when she looks up, that she needs to be comfortable with her surroundings. She started to read, and Glenda said she will see her tomorrow. Ann looked at me with a "What" look on her face!! I told her to listen to her no matter how Dumb it sounds. I told her lets get some sleep; you can deal with it tomorrow. We went to bed this night and slept like a rock. It was before daylight when I awoke in a cold sweat. I had the dream of the War Chief watching as my mother and I fought a battle with the Bear and the Coyote. It sent ice through my blood. I got up and made coffee. I still felt my mothers back touching mine. I shook it off! And went and woke Ann.

It was late in the afternoon when Glenda returned. She pulled a chair up next to me and had her start reading. She was an understanding person with a serious side; and a side that leaves me laughing. As Ann was reading she kept reminding her to look at the light bulb. She got up and told her, that the Bible was the words that bring out the best in us. To speak them with authority. She showed by reading it herself, lifting her arms as she spoke. She had her live in her world as she read. She told her she was preaching it to the world, to put excitement in it, and start looking at the #%#$%###$&*% Light bulb. Then did the goofy eye roll at her. She was laughing so hard she nearly peed herself. She said, "You gotta have fun". Every time she would start to read; she would loose it with her laughter.

Glenda then started thinking. She asked us to come with her to a "Saloon" at the edge of town. She wanted Ann to watch how the girls there perform. I said; "A SALOON" She said yes. She told of the women that work there with sex on their minds. She told Ann of the "carousing and drinking and the filth" Ann started laughing and asked her if she were "Sure of this" Glenda just smiled and told her she doesn't have to "BE" like them, but she needs the "fire" that they show!!

We were standing on the stairway in the saloon when the act started. The women were flipping their dresses in the air and winking at the men, and it was out of control. I was laughing so hard I peed my panties. It then became quiet as the most beautiful woman in the house entered. She started slowly moving through the crowd grabbing men's hats, touching their faces, showing her legs, and just knocking them "DEAD" The tempo picked up and she wrapped her bare leg around a hansom young man; I thought he would faint!! Her voice carried with command of the saloon as she finished her act. She ran to the stage with her arms wide open, with her voice as loud as thunder!! She then fell from the stage as the men gathered to catch her. The place went wild!!! You could feel their hearts "Melting" Ann just stood there with her mouth wide open. She was in "Shock" She turned to me and said; I aint gunna do that" Glenda just smiled and said; "Ya never know!!!"

We were on our way home, when Glenda asked Ann; "Did you feel the Fire"??? Ann was so stunned by the performance, she said; do you have any ICE. Glenda started to laugh and told her she doesn't have to get that carried away with it. She giggled and said she wanted her to see what can be done with the movement, with the smiles, with the connection to the audience!!! It was like she had opened her eyes for the first time. She said "YES" I see what you mean!! Glenda then looked at her body. She told her to throw away her old dresses, that she would dress her like the queen. She said hold your head up girl!!!, demand respect. Demand they listen, and most of all!!! Have fun. "Boy"! I felt Bill talking this night.

The next day, I got out my brass flute and played it softly as she spoke. This seemed to calm her. When it was required I would scream "Put the FIRE in it" She would get a look on her face of "Determination" when I did this. Using her arms, and her hands, she brought me to tears. I was as proud as a mother can be. After two days of practice Glenda returned to us for a reading. She had her work on her mind. She showed her the motions that she made with her arms. She showed when to clench her fist, and when to lift her arms to the sky. She showed her how to lower them slowly with her voice drifting away. She kept moving her head to the light, and would remind her to do this. She said don't look down at anyone till she is done. Two more days had passed when she came back. She now had her bring the words from her chest. She would have her "Near shouting the words with authority, with her arms showing her feelings. She had her speaking softly when the verse required this, with her hands she would ask. She finally got her to look up as she spoke, and had no more reminding her of this. She sat with her and asked her to come to the stage; she gave her the script. Glenda said she now has different words. But to preach them to her when she's ready. Ann asked for a day with the script. Glenda said don't over think it. She wants to hear her speak like its just another sermon. She was looking her straight in her eyes as she said this. She said you "Can" do this girl. Then did that goofy eye roll to Her. You gotta love her!!!

When we got there the next morning Glenda instantly handed her a new script. Ann was starting to protest and Glenda just held her hand up to her and said read!! There were only six of us there. Glenda gave her a moment to read it once before she started. She asked me to play the song of the river while she was reading it. I got out the flute and started. She looked around the stage and then her eyes went to the light. Her voice carried with the wind and the river as she spoke them perfectly. I stopped and looked at Glenda. She said she's on the payroll now!!! I thought she was going to pass out. Glenda then hugged her and gave her the full script; and asked her to be at the rehearsal in two days. We were both just a dancing we were so happy. Glenda handed me the music that she wanted me to play.

The rehearsal was tough on us. She would have Ann lift her arms further make her voice lower, plead till it brought her to tears. She had me put more emphasis on my high notes and go softer on my low notes. She was a slave driver. The only one who knew more then her was God himself. She had everyone to perfection. The show was two days away when we had dress rehearsal. This time though Glenda joined us with her Violin. She inspired the spirit of Ann with her music drifting around her; she gave it all that she had in herself. I could barley play as I watched her. It was beautiful. I had never heard anything like this before. It was like putting music to a spirit. It was like she was singing her script as the words poured from her beautiful lips. She was young and beautiful beyond belief. I was holding her in a bear hug when Glenda came to her and said "Good Job"

We started with half the house full. Glenda said this is what she expected. The next night it was three quarters full and she just smiled. By the fourth night you couldn't even get a ticket to the show, and by the fifth night we were a HIT!!! I took her aside and told her of my memories of a little girl with big ideas. She gave me the Goofy eye roll and said "like that"!!! Oh Boy!!!

She had taught both of us a lesson in this life. She drove us like herding cattle, but she knew when to show us her Love for us. We met more people and had nice friends to dine with each evening. The boys were showing their inetrest in Ann now, and Glenda kept her centered on her job. She told her she's young still. To hold on to the attention they pay to her, but to wait for the one that you cant live without. Then rolled her eyes at her. Oh Man!!

We were so excited!! We RAN to the phone and called Ken. He was a cyiyan and howling with happiness as we told him the news. I asked him if he had gotten the papers back for Ann's adoption yet. He said just today they arrived. I gave the phone to Ann and she was crying the tears of happiness. Glenda was with us and told me she was going to headline the show with "Ann Asher" and play it to the bitter end!!!

A few days went by and I asked Glenda; "What's next" She said when the contract is up she wants to send Ann to school for singing, that she just feels it in her blood. She told me that we had started a new look at the stage, and the old boys that croaked were gone. I had to laugh, She looked to my eyes and she saw it. That I was homesick for Ken and Spokane. She asked me to take care of finding my replacement. She said "Ann Outshines us all" I told her honestly that when she marches across the stage with her violin that she inspires everyone to the top of a mountain, that we would be nothing without her. She held me and said thank you.

I auditioned many people; and hadn't found what I was looking for. Then one day a man came to me with a clarinet. It was a different sound but it caught me by my soul as he played it. I went to the back and got Glenda to come listen to him. When he was done we turned to him and smiled. She said he was what we were looking for. That she will shorten the flute to Ann with the clarinet doing the big job. Ann insisted she use the wood flute, she said she was comfortable with that. She said to keep the use short and she will handle it. I saw her pride and her confidence as it grew every day. I told her that her next appearance was in California and to keep up with Glenda. I told her she lives in my heart and to sing like a bird. I told I feel it. That you will be Famous some day. She said I'll miss you Mom!! I told her to go for it head first, and her Dad and I will be cheering you with every note you sing. To think first of your career and put us second. She was crying tears of happiness as I said goodbye.

Ken asked me to meet him in Montana where the Black Foot tribe was having a gathering. He said He and his Uncle wants to be there. I was excited to be among the nations again and I just couldn't wait to eat fry bread and buffalo meat. MMMMmmm I asked ken of leaving the Fox home this time? He said Mother wont let her out of her site. He said she doesn't want her near the tribes till she understands herself!!!

I ate and danced and just had a ball. It took me back to the days. I cried that Mother and Achak weren't there to enjoy it. Ken said he threatened them with dynamite and couldn't get them to budge. He said they enjoy walking along the river in Spokane and they talk with people they pass. After my third time on the road I knew what they felt. We spent three days there. I asked his uncle if he had picked out a sweet young girl to be his pal?? He said he tried, but they keep telling him he's too old!!! I told him to show them his "Fire." He said he tried that, "and he burnt to the ground" I was laughing so hard that I peed my panties.

Ken came to me this night. He said we had to hurry home. He said he had a message delivered to him that our barn burnt to the ground!!! I shrieked "WHAT" the h---- %%&@#@#%% Seems Fox tipped over a lantern. He said she got the animals out of there though!!! I told him I'm going to ring her little ##$^$$ neck.

We returned to Spokane and I went to Mother and Fox. Fox couldn't face me. Mother told her she's on her own with this one!! Ken asked me to settle down now! I attacked her with a vengeance. As I held her pinning her head to the ground; She said; "I'm sorry" I told her sorry doesn't begin to excuse it. I told her she would spend every minute of every day helping rebuild the barn!!! Ken started to say something. I shut him up with a look from my eyes. Mother shook her finger at Fox, and said; "I told you so" I let her up and told her we are done. She ran away crying. $^@#%$# I was pissed off.

I cooled off after a week of being mad. I still hadn't unpacked my bags. I had so many goodies that I got from the people in Chicago that I think they had to add a car to the train. We spent three days just fussing with that. Mother said you must be popular!! I told her I wasn't half of what Ann turned out to be. She winked at me and said she knew I would figure this out. About this time Fox walked in with a dress on backwards. I laughed so hard I thought I would need stomach surgery!!! I told her to turn it around!! She said "oh" What a little knott head. I was pissed at her. But deep down I love her.

We hired Atsa to help rebuild the #$&^^$% barn. Seems he was fired for shooting Hanyauk with a notice of no re-hire. He told me of being lucky just to get a job for Glen. We were laughing about this. I told him I never figured this out. I asked him how could he be so "loving" to me; and so cruel to a boy that would help him. He said; I don't know!! Its life, and that's just how it goes. He told me of taking the place of his father. I asked how that was working out for him?? He said do remember telling me of the legends?? I said; "Yes"!! That I am still living proof of this! He laughed and said you know what I mean!!! He told of all he went through for the first year that we were gone. He chuckled. He said he is hated by the white! And, the red!! I said join the club. We both tipped over laughing our Butts off. I told him of Ken and the mill. I said he would hire you. He asked how do you know that he would do this for me?? I laughed and asked him; do you think I will leave him a choice??? We laughed so much that it hurt my face!!!

We locked ourselves in the bedroom the first night we were home; and even made Love. It had been so long I thought I would need lessons for this. YEEE HAAA!!! Well?? "Woo -ha" any way. I now followed my sisters barrel racing. The announcer called her "Fox On Fire"; and the poor thing was stuck with it. So I rubbed it in deep. She had a wall full of ribbons that she treasured, and her grades in school had fallen. Mother threatened to sell her horse if she didn't bring them up!!! She was a straight "C" student and that was a miracle she was that. She had her following of Indians and Cowboys that would show up at her door. And they were scared of mother, and disappeared real quick like. Mom was still slim and active and she would look at them with her icy steel eyes. This worked on all but one. This one was "MIKE" He had moved here from Montana when his dad took a job at the Flour Mill. Mom wouldn't allow any trips to the bedroom; she threatened Fox with her hair!! She was starting to show her women-hood with breasts that bulged from her shirt. Mike was helping her with math that she struggled with, as mom came to the room. She dropped her "One Eye" look on Mike as he leaned over her pointing at her papers. With her breast ready to fall out of her shirt Fox was complaining that; "it's Hard" Mike returned the one eye look to mother, and said not as hard as your Mom. She would shake her finger at him and leave the room scowling. I went over and tucked it in for her and she just said "oh;" She was such a sweet little thing!!

After six months of waiting we got a call from "OUR" daughter. Ann was so excited. She was booked at a club in Wisconsin and to be the headline act of that. I begged and pleaded with Ken to go with me!! And he kept talking of work for the mill. I give up and called him Kenasher!! And that changed his toon. He came a grumbling and growling, but when we arrived. He took Ann to his arms and promised to never let go. I knew I had him cornered and stood there with pride. We spent a week there and watched her success. She had gotten over stage fright, and I knew of this myself. With Glenda coaching her I wasn't worried about anything. Except for the young man that held her hand the whole night. I asked Glenda about him!! And she did the eye twirl!! I told her to stop it, and she did it again. By the time I was off the floor from laughing, she said relax that's her coach!! I still wasn't as sure as she was about this, but I was relaxed more since the laughing.

She had changed up the show a bit; she was playing Banjo and guitar for part of her act. But her voice was the key to this. She would hit the notes like a nail on the head. She kept the flute for the end of the show; it was Ann's trademark. The crowd would go absolutely crazy, when Glenda joined her with the violin. We had more fun on this trip then any of the trips that I had made. Just to have Ken there with me made all the difference. Glenda and Ann were going over plans to be a hit in California next. They were on their way. Ken and I went on home. We were so tired; we said woo hoo and went to bed. Damn, I'm feeling my age!!

Ken had left Atsa in charge of the mill while we were gone. He said he had a head for this work; and that he understands the importance of filling the orders. I suggested we invite he and his son for dinner Sunday night. He was happy with the thought of this. Fox and I put a special touch on this. Fox made apple pies for desert. I allowed her to invite Mike with no counsel from Mother. Mother didn't like "crowds" and was unhappy with me for this. I asked her forgiveness and reminded her that Fox is getting to that stage of her life where she needs her friends to help her. She played her flute and thought about it. She said I was right. She said she grew up much faster then I did. I laughed and told her she spends so much time protecting her from this world, that she needs her time to be free. She returned to her flute and thought about this. She said Achak calls her "Stingy" I give her a hug and looked into her eyes; I told her I would never expect any thing less from her!!!

We had the two men over for dinner. We really had a good time. Fox made Glen dance with her, because Mike refused to do this!!! Achak even made Mother dance with him. We just had so much fun.

Glen decided the last dance he would dance with Mother. He bowed to her for the honor of this. He told her she saved his life. I saw a tear in her eye as he spun her around. And he held her tight when they were done with everyone clapping. She said a blessing over him. That Mother is a "Real Lady"

The following week things had slowed down to the pace of an Elk in rut so I could have my time in my crafting room. I could hear mother and Fox a fighting in the kitchen, and Achak came a running out of there. I laid down my project and went to investigate the commotion. Mom was just a chewing on her about her behavior with the boys. I was thinking back to my days when she, well, kind of taught me of that!!! As I watch her shake her finger in her face I started to laugh. Mother asked me what's so funny about this??? I wanted to answer her so bad!!! I told her I had my eye on her and she has done nothing to deserve this. She shouted at her again and said she gave him a kiss. I said I don't think her lips will fall off, I told her to relax and let it go!!! She was on a roll and wouldn't drop it, so I asked her to leg wrestle Fox. She was now quiet and looking at her small frame. Mother said she don't have a chance. I had watched her beat every boy in Spokane, I taught her to do this with a quicker then they are move. Fox looked at her and said "I DARE" yah!! And mother hit the dirt. I told them on the count of three its game on. Mother was just scowling at her and I began the count. When I hit three Mother was upside down and screaming she cheated!! I shook my finger at her and awarded it to the Fox. Mother got up saying @#%(+__&*^% and no have a nice day. She wouldn't talk to anyone for a week. And I loved it. I told Fox to quit sucking the boy's faces. She was giggling and said Mikes a good kisser!!! Oh boy!!! Lay Down Fox; Down!!!

I can't lie and tell you that we were a typical family. I think we were anything but "That" Achak tried to teach at the Spokan reservation and came home disgusted with this. He talked of the Elders whom he dealt with that had no respect for the ways of the whites. I talked to him of the Coeur d'Alene Indians who were much involved with the whites. He had me take him there for a council and, they impressed him. He set up to teach there and Mom wished him well. Mom never went with him, "GEE" I wonder why??? Achak had a great success at the reservation and the kids just loved him. The Elders looked to him for council on their land rights, and he helped by writing letters to Washington for them. They were a family, and Mother never complained of anything after this. Except for her daughter who drove her "CRAZY" She finally retired her lance for a friendship with our neighbors. Her and Bertha would walk and talk most of the days. Bertha had a son and a daughter in school and Fox was a friend of her daughter. She had her eye on her Brother, but we kept her corralled. We had hay wagon rides in the summer, and sleigh rides in the winter. Mother Lozen enjoyed this so much. She had finally found the freedom to just enjoy life. "My Daughter" Ann was busy with her career. She would send us home tokens and trinkets and all kinds of things. She sent us an arrow from the Chippewa - Nation one time, and I just loved the feel of that. I asked her to stop and send one from each tribe she encountered in her travels. Ken staked them to the walls in our house with pride. Mother Lozen walked by and looked at them, and said "Damn" I didn't even see the Indians!!! Bertha and Mother just spent their days at the café in town for coffee and talk. Bertha took her window-shopping one of their trips, and she returned with two dresses for the Fox. Fox was mad and screaming at mother that she has no "Taste" for this. She asked her what was wrong?? She told her that they were old women's dresses!!! She held one looking at it and told her she has no need to show us her breasts. Fox started laughing and told her Mike never complains!!! The WAR was on. I left to do my shopping!!! When I got home it was still going on. I told Fox to calm down and show Mom respect!!! She was saying &^^%$# under her breath. This got me "Mad!!" I told her to just march her Butt back in here and apologize to Mom.! She gave me a hand gesture that was very unbecoming for a girl her age. She pissed me off!!!! I reached out and smacked her right in her chubby little "Chops" She was standing there shaking her head and she started in on me this time!!! I said little sister you done picked the wrong person to talk like that with. I attacked her with vengeance in my heart. Mother was watching with a cup of coffee in her hand and telling me how to fight!!! She started swinging her arm and the coffee was a flying as she was saying "GIVE HER A RIGHT", I finally had her on the floor with my legs wrapped around her and she was struggling for all that she had!!! I told her Mom taught me how to fight, and she did a good job of this!! After what seemed like "Forever" she finally admitted defeat. I made her promise to tell Mom she was sorry before I released her, and she agreed to do this. I released my leg lock on her and she whopped me in the face!!! I grabbed a hand full of her hair and she grabbed a handful of mine and we were back at it again. I shook her hand loose and now had two hands full of her hair and was rubbing her nose into the floor!! Bertha walked in and damn near fainted. Then Mom changed her tune. She said, "now girls you better stop this", in a sweet little voice!!! And I banged her nose on the floor!!! When I looked in the eyes of Bertha she was panicked, crying, and so upset that she was praying!!! I started to laugh. Fox was looking at me and started to laugh too!!! Mother then took Bertha by the arm and told her we were just "Foul little things" That we had better let them settle their differences. I looked at Fox and told her she's foul. She stuck her toung out at me!!! As I was looking at her I was thinking. A typical family? What is that??? She apologized to Mother and I. About a week after this happened. I asked her what brought this on her self. She looked ready to cry when she told me how much she missed her sister Ann. I was thinking, Damn! She could have told me this before we had a boxing match!!! Truth was. I missed her too. I looked at her forehead and told her it was healing!!! She said &(%#@$^# and went to her room

A week later I was walking through town and I stopped and listen to a man play his fiddle. He didn't use the soft quality of a violin but he was making it talk for him. I was watching the people tapping their toes and ready to dance!! as the strings were a popping. I couldn't buy one fast enough. I knew the evil headstrong ways of the Fox all to well. So I took it home and opened the case and placed it on the coffee hutch in the front room. It sat there open for three days. I was starting to worry, when I heard her picking at the strings. I smiled at Ken and he smiled back at me. A week later we heard her using the bow to the strings, and our smiles grew bigger!!! By the end of the month she had it cradled under her chin. We just let her murder her songs. At the end of the second month she asked for help with this. "MAN", What a tuff nut to crack!!! I had been taught the basics of music on several instruments. And spent two months teaching her what I knew. She asked to quit school and take lessons so she could be with her sister. "Alleluia my mother", no more trouble to face with the school. She had an eighth grade education, which was plenty for her. She took to her lessons with a fire in her soul. She would play night and day and play when she went to town. She did a battle of the fiddles with the man on the street and she won the applause of the crowd. Mother was with me this day, as I told her. I said it all comes from you Mother. I saw her smile rise to the sky. She said she always did her thinking while playing the flute. She said I never gave this another thought. The Fox charged at her Mother and they held each other tight. By the end of the eight-grade she was ready to travel.

I was exhausted going through all this. It was Saturday and I asked ken to come to bed with me. I had to get dinner ready for a Sunday chicken dinner and needed the rest. Ken said he was "POOPED" too! We both just collapsed. Ken woke me up with fear in his eyes. He told me I was dreaming. He told me I was choking him. I started crying. I told him of the dream of the Bear and the Coyote. He held me and said nothing.

I talked to Ann and she said she had two weeks left in the east, and her and Glenda would come to Spokane and see what the Fox has!!! She made me feel a part of her, when Ann told me she needs some "Mom time". Ken booked Fox at his favorite tavern. She had a ball playing there for the crowd. They had dancing and drinking and they just got wild. It was fun in any mans language. I asked when she was done if she had any problems?? She said her "BOOBS" got in her way!!! I told her she's on her own with that one!!! She had Mother cut some material and they wrapped them up tight. I "ran" from the room laughing. Mother came to me and told me she can always find work as a wet nurse if her music doesn't work out!!! Forgive me Fox. We laughed our butts off!!! The next day Mike showed up. He took a long look at her. He turned to me and asked if we had any milk. OH MY GOD!!! I still haven't stopped laughing. Sorry Fox.

I was working in the craft room when Ken came home. He was looking for Fox to take her to town. I told him to check at the barn, and see if her horse is there. I was working on a embroidery project and didn't want to stop. Well!!! I stopped, when Ken came back to the house. He had caught Fox and Mike in the barn making happy times with each other. It shot through my mind; do I tell Mother? Or handle this for her. I asked Ken where are they at now? He said he was so mad at her, he told them not to move, that they needed a talking too!!! I was looking at him and said you mean this falls on me!!! He said do you really think she will have a neck left after your Mother gets done with her?? After a long look at him, I said your coming with me! He said you damn right I'm coming with you!! He was so pissed off that he could barely talk. He was a man of honor, He never asked me to do anything till I was ready. I was worried about Ann all this time, and now it's the Fox that gets my attention. I looked at Ken and asked him "how long has this been going on." He was so "pissed", he said they have been together for three years now!! I asked him to relax, that we have to think this out before we open our mouths. He said he never thought Mike would do this to her. I started shaking my finger at him. I asked him what makes him think this was Mike's idea?? He had a pants to tight look on his face. He said, you think this was her doing?? I said "I Know This Was Her Doing" He instantly said %*^()()&#()&%$#. He was just crushed by this. I asked him to talk to Mike and I will talk to Fox. I wasn't ready for this. I had nothing to compare it with, the way I was raised!! Well; forget it!! Ken was right though. Mother had done a complete turn around since she had married Achak. And if Achak gets hold of her he will kick her butt to the stars!! I didn't know what to say to her.

Ken took mike to town with him. I sat and looked to her eyes. I asked her how long has this been going on??? She said she was seventeen now, and feels she's grown enough to understand how this works. I asked her if she were ready to raise a child at seventeen?? She said "YES" if it happens then she is ready, but that she keeps track of her cycles and she doesn't; think it's a problem. I had to admit, I wasn't expecting that answer, I asked her if he forced himself on her?? She smiled the size of the sun and told me, that she nearly tore his pants off to get him to do it!!! That he wasn't sure if it was right!!! She went on to tell me of her and Mike talking to the Elders at the reservation. I asked her what else she had learned from them??

She told of meeting her "Blood" Father!!! She told this was about a year and a half ago. She told me this was part of an agreement between her father Achak and the Chief. She said it was after he took the job as a teacher for them. She said she was scared to meet him. She started to smile as she spoke of Achak. She said he stood by her side and never let go of her hand. She spoke of the Chiefs "Wisdom" She said he was a mighty man. She said he asked her only one question. She looked up at me: and said he asked her "who is her father"?? She said she was scared and hid behind Achak and peeked around him to look at the chief. She said she would never forget his smile!!! She showed me the little Gold cross that he gave her. She said it was to remind her to honor her Father. She started crying again telling me she had dishonored her father Achak. I held her and told her he will forgive you. I told her even though he seems to be "perfect" that I'm sure he will understand. I told her I just pray that Mike shows his Love for you as much as Achak does!!! She sat up and said she never thought about this before. She said she needs both of them for their love. She admitted not knowing of our mothers love!! She said she's waited a lifetime to hear her say she loves her. I smiled and asked if she felt it?? She looked at me and said yes. I pinched her nose and told her that's all she will ever say!!! That she was brought up in the old ways of life, She shows us but never speaks of it. I told her it's like the story of the girl and her kitten. Not a word was spoken between them; but you could still feel the Love between them. It was like I opened her eyes.

She smiled and told me of using the tribel laws to marry them. I asked her if she had talked of this with her Elders?? She said she tried, but it just turned into a fight. I was unprepared for this. She said "sister" you were much younger than me when you went through this. I asked what she knows of this?? She told me of Mother crying one night and she was asking forgiveness for what she put you through!! She said she didn't go into details, but she said she was following a way of life where it was "Natural" to do this. I was unsure what to say. I asked how long she has been married to him? She said nearly a year now. I asked her why she had hidden this from me!! That I am her sister and she should have had counsel before she married him. She said I sounded like Mike now, that she had counsel with so many Elders that she was fed up with it!!! She said she was waiting for a quiet time to talk to me, but that it's never quiet in our house. I gave her a hug, and said you got that right!! I told her she was coming with me to tell mother of this when I'm ready!! She quietly said good luck with that!! I wanted her to understand our Mother. I broke my vow and told her of Mothers promise that you will never see the bloodshed that we went through. She wants to hold you safely away from this. She asked if the rumors are true?? I didn't answer.

I asked her if she still wanted to follow her sister to the road of her music?? She said she would like to try it, she said she didn't care if it worked out or it doesn't. She said she will be happy to be with Mike weather she's on the reservation or sitting in a fancy café!!! I asked what Mike thought of her trying out for the job?? She smiled and said, He promised to wait for her. I knew Mike pretty well now, and I had no doubts about this. I asked her if the people at the flour-mill knew of this?? She told me they were all there for the ceremony!! I said shame on you I would have been there for you!!! She giggled and said Mike was her priority at this time, that if she had to wait any longer that she would have tied him to the barn and teased him till he did this for her. Oh Man, times have changed. I asked her of Mike's parents, and what they thought of this? She said they gave them a blessing a year ago. The last thing I faced was Mother Lozen. I told her it will break her heart to tell her of this. She said, "I know it" She said she just couldn't wait. I had a thought enter my mind. I asked her if she would use the white mans church to marry Mike, like Ken and I had done? She said "THAT'S WHAT SHE WANTED when all this (&^&%%$%^ started. I said "oh" I told her I will talk to Ken about this. She told me she tried to talk, but he was so pissed off at her that he couldn't even talk!! I laughed and told her I'll handle this. I said I need to talk to Ann about this too. She said she knows of this, that she wished me well!!! I thought, *&*(*)%&^$#

When Ken got back from town, we both said &(^%&^^(^@@$^$&^+&*^ and a few more un-colored words. Ken was looking at me with his teeth clenched tight and a look on his face that would stop a charging Buffalo!!! And I started to LAUGH. I told him we are just a typical family!!! I was wishing I could roll my eyes like Glenda does. He finally said "crap" he then said, "crap, crap, crap." I reminded him of our getting together on the road after I started with Music!! He smiled as he thought about this. He told me of his demanding that they be married properly in a church. I said she wanted that in the beginning!! And he said I KNOW this NOW!!! He was upset more that Mother Lozen doesn't know, and he felt as low as a snake to tell her. I told him I will tell her. He looked at me and said unless I sing it to her that I would trip on my words and get her confused, and he would be doing double duty to fix that!! I said "oh" He was right. I told him I will go with him and keep my mouth shut while he talks!! He asked that he could bring a pair of dirty socks to put in my mouth if I should try to speak??? I laughed and said I promise!! He said he will carry a clean pair.

We went before, "The Warrior Lozen." With her steel gray eyes on us, Ken began to talk. He "lost it". He dropped to his knees just shaking his head. I said the Fox is married. She laughed and said she knows of this. Ken looked at her and said "WHAT"??. She said she uses her silence to torture her with this, that she will punish her with this till she tells her the truth!!! She told me of Kumbah's sister who refused to take a vow of silence, that she ran to her and spilled her guts to her. Ken said #%&$%&&*(_^(^*%%^ and got up and left us. I started laughing. Mother did too. I said "Shame on you mother" Tee Hee. I put on my "Tough" face and told Mother Lozen that I would send the Fox to her for counsel. She said, "Bring it on" I marched to the door with determination in my soul and opened it ready to speak!!!

And Ken was standing there with a pair of socks in his mouth. And I lost it. I just looked at Fox and pointed at the door. I nearly erupted a blood vessel holding it back. I RAN to the kitchen and laughed till it hurt. Ken stepped in behind me and said, Caannn III hheeeellppp yyyoouu mmaaammnn. I pulled the socks from his mouth and gave him a kiss. Then put them back in. I told him, "WE are just a normal family" Mike poked his head in the door and asked Ken to come with him, that he had something he wanted to show him. They left the house and I went back to the craft room. After two hours Fox came and sat with me. She laid head on the table and looked like the Bear had just got done with her for dinner. I said Mother won the battle didn't she??? She said "yes" The poor kid was hurting. I gave her a hug and told her this will pass. She started to honestly cry and asked for my forgiveness. I held her and told her I see the heart of a warrior in her. I asked her not to look behind her, but to pick up her feet and move forward, that maybe she is right too!!! She just sat quietly as I held her. I asked her to start dinner, that I would clean up the craft room and be there to help her. She had nothing to say as she left the room.

Achak said grace and we started to pass the food around. Mother asked Fox to pass her the gravy. As she was handing it to her, Mother took her by her wrist. And smiled at her. She said it all with her steel gray eyes. And a smile was on the little fox as she looked at her. I felt like we were a normal family now. Everyone took a deep breath and the table talk started. Ken told me of the land that Mike had bought to build them a house. He said it was about two miles down stream from us. And the talk went on with comfort in our hearts. I brought up the fact that Ann would be here next week. Fox was looking at Mike and said she hates to see her; that she decided to stay here to help mike with building their house. Mother looked at her and told her this is the wise of you my daughter; you have used your head for a change. Mother then asked when she will be Grand Mother?? She had a way with words!!! Fox said not till the house is done.

Ann came home and learned of the news. That her sister wouldn't be going with her. Fox said lift up your face sister, and I will show you the way to have "Fun" She booked the tavern for her act this night, and grabbed her fiddle and ran. We were sitting front seat as she charged onto the stage with the music coming franticly at us, and suddenly it stopped. She stared at the audience and asked a man what he's looking at!! The man laughing said a little "Red" girl. She said you damn right I'm red!! That you white bastards squeezed the land out of us and our skin turned this color!!! And she returned to her music with a fervor!!! She suddenly stopped again, and asked a man why he's white!!! He looked around and said I don't know. She laughed and told him it's because a warrior squeezed the shit out of him!!! And she was back into her music just playing and dancing with the music just a flying around. Glenda was laughing so hard that she nearly choked to death. She stopped her music again and asked Glenda why the white girl was laughing. Glenda just stood there laughing and reached a hand to her. She told her to shit in that one and look at the other and tell her which one was full!!! She then took to the music with the whole place in stitches. She had a bag full of one-liners. I was ready to call for an ambulance. She finished her set with, All you white bastards have a good evening. And the applause thundered through the city. Even Mother was laughing. Ann was in tears, and said she will never top that one!!! I think we laughed for three days. Glenda told her if she ever changes her mind. To come see her first!!! Yup, just a typical family!!! Glenda took a poster down that said "FIRE FOX" and put it in a tube. She was holding it rolling her eyes. She said it would be a few years before the audience was ready for her, but look out world she's a coming!!!

The following year I was bringing the kids lunch. They were nailing the shingles to the roof. They had worked so hard at building their home that it made me shine with pride. I asked her if I hear little footsteps in her house??? She said she wasn't sure of this yet, that Glenda was still in touch with her asking the same question. I told her I was jealous of her, that I can never do this with a child for myself. She asked if I had considered adoption? I said yes, but told her I want to hold the one who comes from our Mother. I told her I was "Stingy" She said yes, you are that!! She giggled and talked of when she was young. That she had me wrapped around her fingers. I stuck my toung out at her!!! I told her I felt like her mother, and her sister. She said Thank God for that. Mike was climbing back to the roof, and she said I will be the first she talks to if she decides to try it. I patted her hand and went home.

A month later she was at my door. She told me of the "Hans and Nix comedy routine in California now playing with the heading of "Fun, Music, and Song" She was telling of how it was a hit there. She talked of six girls who do this routine and of how she feels it tugging at her Soul. She told me of talking to Glenda about this, that she said Glenda could never copy the look of a judge on my face for the whole routine that I had done. I told her that her whole family is in show business now, and there is always room for another. I told her I started it in desperation to save you and Mother, with no idea where it would take me. She said this means waiting for a baby!! I wanted to cry, but told her it's her choice, that I will be behind her till she is done. She was thinking. She asked if I would come with her?? I said I don't know about that. She walked off saying I made the decision for her. I started crying. I wanted to kick my stingy old ass. I hollered come back here, and we will talk to Kenasher and see what he says. She was laughing and said "KENASHER" I told her it might come to that to get permission. I was sick. I "was" going to go to Colville and see Nalin. Fox is my true sister; she comes first.

I told her to copy every move I make. We went to the kitchen and we dropped to our knees. We clasped our hands tight. I said may I have a moment King Ken; I have a request that I would like to ask of thee!!! Fox had a look on her face that would stop a freight train. I said sir, may you show us your grace with this request that we make, for with our hearts that we lay them before you and pray you are kind.

Ken was looking at us and said what in the hell are you two up too now???

Fox took over now. She said oh; may you see the distress that wraps round my heart King Ken; It tears at my Soul just to say!!! That I need my sister to travel with me, and I pray!! that thou don't say nay.

"I thought, what the hell is NAY" sounds like what a horse says!!!

Now Ken was getting into this. He said, "Rise" to your feet my Red daughter, tell the white Father more when I say!!! That I feel your heart failing, and I see your eyes pleading. What is it you ask me to say???

I got up and took a back seat for this one.

With her hands still clasped. She begged him please King Ken that I ask you not for money, For I know you have a heart made of gold. I would give you all of my riches if you don't tan my britches, for I ask only your wisdom only today!!!

He said; Lo my red daughter you strike me with flattery, I feel thou trying to make smooth the way!! You do this so well that how in the hell, can I offer my opinion, when I know not the land I then say!!! What treasure you ask for, and the land that you travel is a "Question" unanswered, I say, with a slight slip of dismay!!!. I see the gloom! So as I stand in this room!! Get a broom and sweep it AWAY!!!

I got up and left. They were just---"RIDICKULOUS"

I put on a pot of coffee and was having my first cup by the time they joined me. King Ken said; may your journey be swift my Queen "XA'XAT'S" that he gives his permission to GO!!! The Fox was dancing and so happy!! I just shook my head. I thought people go to town to see THAT!!!

We were on the rail again. Headed for California. Fox set it up with Glenda to meet us and join us for her appearance. Seems Glenda had become a talent scout for the music industry. The woman was crazy. Mother was laughing when we left. Seems Fox practiced her one-liners on her. She said if she can make mother laugh. I told her "I get it" I was pissed that a joke was more important then a "baby".

The Fox gave up. She handed me my flute. She dug out her fiddle and started to play. Every head turned and she told a quick joke. And she started the song of the Bear and the Coyote. And she was just smiling at me. She made her fiddle talk, and slowed it to the music. And I joined in with the flute as she played. She took me back to the start of this. To my days in Colville. I felt my stingy heart melting. I saw the little girl. I listen to her talent. I started crying. She understood this. We ended the song with a hug. I told her I was sorry. And the applause drown out the sound of the train.

When we arrived I saw Ann there with Glenda and ran to her as fast as I could. She told me that she bought out her contract, that she wouldn't miss this for anything in the world. I was crying and I looked at Glenda and said; I wish Bill was here to see this" and her eyes welled up with tears. We went to our room in the hotel. We talked this night of Bill. Glenda told me she modeled her life after him, that he taught her how to capture the music. And the people that use it with a talent for pursuing it. With a talent for just being who they are. I looked at her. And agreed. The Fox showed up in a slick looking dress from Paris, and said lets get going. Glenda was giving her a talk about not having a rehearsal. The Fox just laughed, and told her she has to read the audience!! And how are going to rehearse for that??? Glenda did her coo coo eye twirl. The Fox just looked at her with a serious face and asked her if she were ready!! Glenda looked at me and said "yes"

We went to the Palladium and it was a packed house for the Hans and Nix crew. The Fire Fox was their opener. And she knocked them dead. She took off from the stage and was playing in the audience. She stopped suddenly and put her bare leg in the lap of a man and rubbed her hand down her leg and asked him to touch it!! With a smile on her face. He reached out and touched it with his finger. She grabbed his Bolo tie and said, "Hang him" She just spent her whole time among the audience teasing and taunting the men. Glenda said lets all go help her at the end of her act. Me with my flute. Ann on the piano. And the fiddle and the violin on stage. I started the song, of the bear and the Coyote. We all hit every note to perfection. And the hall stood quiet!!! As we ended the music. And the roar started growing and the applause was like thunder. And didn't stop till we left the stage. One of the girls from the Hans Nix crew looked at us and asked to join the opener!!! Fire Fox was a hit. Glenda smiled and named us as "Sisters" I told Glenda like Bill said. "IM OUTTA HERE" I was ready to go home. Glenda asked of Nalin. I told her there's still trouble brewing up there. I told of her living scared to death of the men that watch them. She asked if she ever left the reservation? I told only if she sets it up with the sheriff. She said God Bless him. I told her it's not fair. That she is my sister too. We said goodbye and I returned home.

Nalin was on my mind. Ken and I went to see her after a week. She was a train wreck. I asked her Mother again if I could take her with me. She just cried and refused my offer. We went back to Spokane. Ken asked me if I had any more dreams. I just nodded yes to him. I told him I get them more often now; and I see it clearer each time. He held me tight.

A few years had gone by, and the Fire Fox returned to us. She took a break to have a baby; and I cried. When she was born to the loving Fox!!! I saw her beauty. With her fathers high cheekbones; and the steel gray eyes of her Grand Mother. And the evil little smile of her mother. Mom and I would share her more, but we are stingy. We let her mother have her when she was hungry. And then they threw us out!!! Stingy little; !@#%!@##$@#$

Mom and I bought books with baby names in them with deep study on the names giving their meanings and the countries of origin and just everything you would ever wish to know of this. And they named her "Amy" %&$%$#@^#%^%^&)(_*&$

Not everything goes the way you want it too!! But we love her. Things settled down to the roar of a cannon now. We just lived life day by day. Mom was busy being a Grand Mother now, and her and Achak would steal Amy and take her to town. With their arms full of bottles and blankets, they had a ball showing her off to their friends. As I sat thinking about this; the thought of Nalin entered my head. There was no way to contact her on the reservation, and I missed her. The sheriff brought her to town on Saturdays so she could play the piano. Her Mother hung onto her with a death grip. She only allowed the sheriff to take her there to do this. I had heard nothing for two months. I begged King Kenneth to ride along with me, and he said "CUT THROAT HEVAN" and we left. I had the wagon master pull up to the tavern in town, and we listen for music from the stage as we waited. It was quiet this afternoon, and I told him to move on. We went to the stables and rented a buggy. While Ken was hooking up the horses, He asked of stopping at the tavern? I told him I was hoping to hear the piano; and of the lady I hired to teach her. I told him she had returned the checks that I wrote for this. He said this sounds odd!! I said we have enough daylight to ride to the reservation, that I felt that we should. He finished loading our poles and our luggage. He looked at me smiling and told me that I'm beautiful when I'm "worried", he asked that we stay in town for this night. He said if we can't find her we have no lodging, and we have the wrong color skin to ask. I had forgotten that I was white. He asked of the checks that were returned? I told him it happened twice. I thought I had overpaid her for her teaching and it made me curious when it happened twice. He jumped in the wagon and said lets go fishing and talk about this; he said we would stop for a room for the night. We stopped at the boarding house and got our room. I asked of Nalin and they had heard nothing from her, like they didn't know who she was!! My heart sunk to the bottom of the ocean as we left there, I was worried!! And my heart was doing flip-flops as we headed to the river. I was fidgeting with my bait as we sat by the river. I told ken that I feel something "Bad" He asked me to relax.

We went to bed this night and my feelings were strong. Like listening to the wind in the hills. I felt my blood returning to the days of war with the white men, and the red men I never slept a wink this night. I was up early the next morning as I returned from the kitchen. I made a pot of coffee to start the day. Ken was still in bed when I asked him to drink this, and went to hitch up the horse to the buggy. Ken grabbed our poles as we left town, He asked me to settle down. I told him now that I'm here, that I feel something wrong. He understood me and cracked the whip at the horse. It was early morning as we arrived with the tribe glaring at us I rushed to Nalin's lodge; I beat on her door and demanded an answer. I heard her voice say! "Who's out there" and I yelled it's your sister Xa'xats!! And she opened the door crying. She was holding her brother just scared to death.

She gave me the information I needed. She spoke of her new father riding to Gold Hill to stop the young braves from getting in trouble for rustling the cattle that they sold them, that his contract was no good. She said her father was arrested for this as things got out of hand. I asked of the young braves? She said she thinks they went to Canada. She told me of a man who testified against her father, she said it was a pack of lies. My blood was boiling as I asked where he lives. Ken said, "your not going there". I asked Ken to look over her, that I just wanted to talk to some people about this. He kissed me goodbye and said be careful. I unhitched the wagon and rode like the wind to Gold hill. The men were gone tending the cattle. Just a few standing guard at the gate. I looked white and they saw no problem letting me pass. The rancher stepped to the railing on his deck and was leaning on it, as I asked him why he lied?? He snarled to get out of here! I picked up a piece of firewood and smashed his fingers to the rail. As he was stumbling around I took his knife from his scabbard and held it to his throat. He was unprepared for what was happening. I made a slight knick and promised to go deeper. He was screaming asking why I was doing this, that he's just an Indian!! I told him my name and his eyes grew larger, and his wife was at the door. I told her to bring all his weapons out here right now. I banged his head on the rail and knocked him out. I told his wife to saddle his horse. She ran to the barn as I picked up his weapons and I threw them into the pond. I tied his hands behind his back and his wife helped him onto his horse. I told her his lies, may have cost a man his life. On the way out I kicked the guard in his face, we rode back to Colville as fast as I could, leading the horse he was mounted on; he hung tight to the backrest on his saddle. As I rounded the corner the town was stirring. A man was throwing a rope over the maple tree with Nalin's father in tow. I rode close to him and kicked him in the face. Three men went to grab me and got the same. The sheriff stepped forward and told me of his conviction for cattle rustling. The crowd was angry at my stopping them and I shouted to listen to what the man tied up has to say!!! They all looked to him tied up and I went to his side. He looked to my eyes of fire as he admitted that he hadn't really seen him before, that he's just an Indian!! He then shouted. "What difference does it make"? Nalins mother was screaming at him now in her native language and he kicked her in her face. I pulled him from the horse and I let him have it in his face. The sheriff broke it up and told the people to go home. They left in silence to their actions with one man protesting that he would hang him anyway. I picked up a shovel that leaned on the tree. I beat him so badly that he never got to his gun. The sheriff said that's "enough now" and took his gun from his belt. He placed us all under arrest and took us to jail. I apologized for the way I had acted as we were walking to the jail. He was an honest man of his word and said he will have the judge come to hear us, that he suspected something was wrong. He told me of Nalin when she played the piano at the bar. I told him she's a good girl who just wants to be left alone. He talked of the man that I tied up getting drunk and bothering her, that he removed him from the bar twice. I spit on the ground and told him he's a piece of crap. He laughed and told me I was very lady like!! I started to laugh at myself. As he locked us up he was yelling at "Mister Johnson" to shut up, and his wife stood there crying. He took her back with him to the front. I poured a glass of water and threw it at him and told him to shut his mouth. Every time I would do this he just got louder, and I threw everything I could find at him. The sheriff came in and unlocked his door; and conked him over his head. He then asked me if I wanted anyone contacted. I told him of leaving Nalin and Ken at her lodge. He said he's not allowed to ride there without a warrant for some ones arrest. He told me the warrant that he had expired. Then smiled and said it wont take long for this to get out of the bag!! Sure enough!! The little family arrived and we had a counsel!!!

Mister Johnson was still screaming that he wanted to talk to his wife. Ken walked to his cell and grabbed his collar, and banged his head against the bars. I was laughing at him as Nalins mother thanked him. I spit as hard as I could past my bars!! Ken said don't waste your spit on him and we were both laughing. He said my legend was out of control. I apologized to him, and he said it's all right. He said at least this one walked away!! He walked back and looked at his face! He said barely, "but he walked away".

I asked Ken to take them home and let them get some rest. Nalins mother was about to fall. The sheriff let her go. I said I was furnished with the finest bunk in town. He said it's the "Ritz" and collected the family. I made him promise me to sleep on the light side this night. He looked at me and asked if there were a problem? I told him of the man determined to hang him because he's just an Indian. He asked if I packed a pistol? I said I never use them. He said he would be back in a moment and went and bought one. He talked to the sheriff and they all left the jail. I had calmed down now and lay on the bunk. I heard Johnson moaning and told him to shut up. And it was quiet in here for the night.

I was talking with Nalins father who went by the name "White Feather" and he told me of all that had happened. He told me of the man who wanted to see him hung is involved in this some how. He described it as legal rustling when the white man makes a deal with an Indian and his cattle leaves the reservation!! They are not allowed to take them to court. He told me unless they demand money on the spot; that it always winds up this way. I asked him why the young warriors traded with this man? He said they were drunk when they did this. He told me of the whites that bring alcohol; to the young and the old to bring out the coyote in them. The sheriff stuck his head in the door and told us he was going to make his rounds. He said if we need anything he was leaving his deputy here. I saw White Feather get nervous as the sheriff closed the door. I asked him what was wrong??? He said the deputy is part of this. I got up and was looking for a weapon. I saw a broom next to the door, and that was it. Shortly after the Sheriff left, he deputy came in and unlocked the doors and told us to "RUN" He handed Johnson a gun and, and went to forcing White feather out of his cell. I was walking to the door and grabbed the broom from the corner and jabbed him right in his eye. I hauled off and kicked Johnson so hard, that he lay there crumpled on the floor. White feather managed to knock out the deputy. We drug them into a cell and locked the door on them. White feather was ready to run. We each took a gun and we waited for the sheriff, I told him I trust him! to just relax. I told him if we run now we will never stop running. We sat in our cells with the doors open, and kept everything calm. They started to get noisy so we stuffed their mouth with their handkerchiefs and tied their hands to their feet to the bars in their cell. I asked white Feather of the one who wished to hang him, I asked if he lived in town. He said he thought so but that he didn't know. I told him I feel him slithering like a snake. I told him to hide his gun under the pillow and be ready to use it. We swung our doors shut but left them unlocked. About twenty minutes had passed and we heard the front door open. I told White feather to be ready. The man stepped in the back, with a look of disbelief on his face. He came to their cells just a cussing and swearing and raised a gun to my face. I was standing there holding the door, and I kicked the door open, and the man still had his gun. I bit a chunk from his ear as I wrestle. White Feather conked him over his head with his pistol. He apologized! and told me he was Christian. I thanked him for telling me this "NOW" We locked him up with the others and I took White Feathers pistol, and laid them both on the Sheriffs desk. I asked him if this is "ALL" He said I think so!!! I shook my head and said %%^)_*&^%# to him. He smiled and said you are welcome!!!

I kept the broom in my cell and prayed not to use it. I thought this is sad that I only have a **&^$^$% broom. I would trade my underwear for a lance if I could. The door swung open and in walked the Sheriff, He said WHAT THE HELL!!!! I said calm down and I'll tell you a story!!! He said "Well"; I want to hear this, as he looked at his deputy's eye. I told him of all that had happened and I told him of my feelings, that I am worried that there is to be more. He listens to me talking and went to his deputy and put his foot on his throat as he talked. He admitted that there were more of them, but of course he didn't know where they were. I asked him to draw up a writ for White Feathers arrest, and we will ride to the reservation to find them. He asked why the reservation?

I told him of sending Ken there with Nalin's family there. He asked me about talking with the rancher. I told him of the scuffle with the guards. He said we better hurry! White Feather said I "aint" staying here so he came to ride with us. The sheriff gave him a gun, and he laid it down. I told him, he doesn't believe in those nasty things. I took both guns with me and rode like the wind.

We were about half way there. The sky was turning dark. Lightning struck the ground in front of me about a hundred yards ahead of us. And the thunder rolled over the mountain. The horses were bolting under all of us. I felt the Great Spirit put the wind to our backs, and the horses ran till they were worked up with lather!!!!

I had waited a lifetime for this moment in time!!!

"As the thunder and lightning rolled over the mountains"

When we got there it was pandemonium with guns firing, and people just running for cover. White feather grabbed him a club and said he would work to the west. The Sheriff shook his head and told him to go!! He asked me to work to the east and he would give us cover fire, so I gave him one of my guns. He opened up with wall of bullets flying as we took to their flanks. I was crawling towards them watching White feather doing the same. One of them seen me; and the lead started flying, I saw White feather lower the boom on the man. He never picked up a gun as he worked his way tighter to them. I rolled over and shot one of them in his leg. The fire was directed at me now. White Feather moved closer. I rolled to the ground and emptied my pistol, and hollered at Ken to see if he was ok. He said he was fine; but Nalins mother was bleeding! as a bullet whistled by my head. I shouted how many are out here?? He said I think ten of them. I asked where the tribel police were? He said they are dead. I was thinking, you dirty **&%$#@ son of a bitch!! I hollered to the Sheriff that we still have seven of them. I heard his big shot gun go off with a boom. He said there are six of them now. They all started firing and were walking towards us, with the lead falling like rain. White feather came up from behind them with two shotguns that he picked from the ones that fell. When he opened up on them there were bodies just falling. White Feather kept pulling the trigger as they fell. His guns were empty when the sheriff unloaded, and the blood was thick in the air. White feather ran to the mother as the sheriff and I checked out the men that we shot, to make sure this was it. Ken had wrapped her leg with a sheet from the bed, and used his belt to tourniquet her wound. When I walked in ken was showing Nalin how to use pressure to slow the bleeding. He was checking her for other wounds. He was near crying when he looked at me and told me she wouldn't take cover. Ken said her son was hit first and she panicked. I looked to the back and saw White Feather holding the limp body of his son. He walked outside and held him up to the sky. Chanting the death song as he held him. I told the Sheriff I would find a wagon to take the mother to town. The tribe was now looking at what had happened. I asked if anyone else was hurt. There were two people hit in the raid. The men brought round a wagon, and we loaded them up. The sheriff led the way. We left White Feather there. He was holding his son. The tribe gathered around him and the drums were sounding, and the pain struck deep in my heart. I asked Nalin how long has this been going on?? She cried, for six months now. She said her father has been trying to stop this for "Six Damn Months"!!! I felt like pukeing. Ken took over her mother and sent Nalin to me. I held her tight. She kept asking; "Why" did he have to die??? I had no answers for her.

The hospital staff met us out front. They went to work on her as fast as they could. After a while, Ken told me to take Nalin to our room. He said he would stay and keep watch over her. I told Nalin, lets go home. She was crying and said she don't want too!! I told her that Ken will be here with her mother, and these things take time. To come home with me and we will pray. I just wanted her to get away from this. She cried all night.

The next morning I got a message from Mother Lozen. It read Ill be there as soon as I can. I thought how in the world did she hear of this. Nalin was asleep now and she needs the rest. I got another message from Achak; that read, "I will pick you up at your quarters at the fort" Mother and Achak both know that I don't have anything to do with the forts. I asked the man that brought the message to me, if the Captain was in at the fort? His eyes grew large as I said this! And I knew this thing was out of control. The word got around after meeting the

Captain at fort Sherman that I was threatening and vulgar. I decided to wait outside the gates at the fort, looking as Indian as I could get!!!

I woke Nalin up and started asking questions. She mostly wouldn't answer me. I told her that I feel the danger of this crawling cross the ground like a snake!! She was just looking at me. I asked her whom she taken the vow of silence for!! She wouldn't answer. I was just looking at her trying to figure out a way into her mind!!

I asked her of "Frau Mia Weber" and told her of the checks that were returned!! I watched as the tears rolled off her face. I asked her if she was still at her ranch? She just shook her head "No" I would never ask her to break her "vows" to her people. I had made vows to my mother that I still respect. I felt this thing "growing" I needed to get by the general store, and I was near ready to go. Something told me to be careful with this. I pulled back the curtain a bit and looked to the street out front. I saw two men with iron on their hips standing across the street from us, "Just watching" I asked Nalin to stay there that I would just be gone for a minute. She was nervous now and I told her not to move. I went to the back, and spotted a man there too. I came back to Nalin and told her, "I need to get out of here", She became upset again, and I asked her for her help. She was nervous but agreed to help me. I asked if she knew of anyone else here at the boarding house that lives here that she trusts. She thought a bit, and said Mister Riley lives here, that she knew him from the tavern. We went to his room and he was passed out drunk. I told her this was a friend she could live without. We stole his cloths from him and I put them on. I dug in his pockets and found two dollars. We stuffed the clothing with pillows so they fit. "Kind of"

I pulled my hair up under the hat, and threatened her with her life if she left his room. I told her not to go back to the room that we had in our name, that it's not safe there now. She asked where I was going? I didn't want to tell her incase someone should capturer her. I told her, "For a look around"

I stumbled out the back way and wasn't noticed. I went to the edge of town where the Indians were, and traded the gun for my clothing. I went next to the general store to buy the iodine that I needed, and listen to two of the men in there who were talking. They were grumbling

about the Sheriff and the tribe. I bought a box of bullets and a bottle
of iodine and left the store. I went to the hospital and asked to have
Ken sent out to talk to him. The lady that helped me was suspicious
and I kept my head low. I took him to the side and told him what I had
learned. As I was speaking I noticed a man in the hallway that had
his eyes on us. I was shaking Kens hand and passed the bullets to him
and told him I would bring him another weapon. He nodded his head
and said, "Be careful"

I went back to the boarding house with a swagger in my step. I
walked close enough to the men who watched us so I could identify
them if needed. As I walked by the man in the back of the house I
noticed his leg bleeding. This told me that I could trust the doctor
in town. If they were still bleeding from the last battle, they were
becoming desperate!! I went in the back way and knocked on the door
and whispered that it was I!! There was a man at the door to our room
leaning against the wall. I told her of this and went to dressing as a
squaw. I covered my face and hands with the Iodine as Nalin fixed my
hair into pigtails. She rubbed the soot from the stove into my hair.
Mister Riley started to wake up. I grabbed a bottle of whiskey and had
Nailin pour him a drink. It wasn't long and he was passed out again.
I told her to keep him "Drunk" I loaded the pistol and told Nalin I
needed one more trip to town. I told her if she heard knocking on the
door to hide under his bed!!

I left his room scowling in "Sahaptin" with my hand on the pistol
and wandered from his room. I saw him move to the door of Riley and
lean against the wall. I went to the hospital and found the window
to Nalin's mother's room. Ken came and opened the window and I
passed him the pistol. I told him the stage will be here in around an
hour, that I had to meet mother and Achak at the fort. He told me of
the man asking questions of the doctors and nurses whenever they left
her room. He told me that he had talked to them of this and of how
they just tell him there is no change in her recovery. I asked him how
she was doing?? He just shook his head. He then smiled and told me I
was a good-looking red skin!!! I whopped him and said Yah-Teh-Hey.

I sat with the tribe outside the fort. One of the older female Elders
recognized me and came and sat with me. She looked to my eyes and

told me I was Xa'xats, that I was "Chaske" (or first born) of the Lozen. I asked how she knew of this. She talked of the times in Colville when the woman of "Wasna" stirred up the wind. I told her that the wind is stirring again, that it brings the blood of the white man with it. She sat there with her head going up and down. She told me of contact with my mother. She told me that only the women of the tribe might move now; that what few men that were left are watched. She nodded her head to the east and showed me the two men who were watching us. She told me of the sub Chiefs passing and of how the white rancher made sure there was no new Chief to take his place. She talked of the brave ones who rode from the reservation to find help with this, never returned. She said look at who sits here with us. That it's only the women and a few children. I told her I see this, that I feel her sorrow. I asked her if the Bear still growls in her heart for her loss. She said he tears at the sole of all the women!! I asked her how many bears she can count on for help? She looked up at the few that were there and said if she spoke with them, that I could count on them all for their help. She just looked at me and said, "What can we do"

I told her of my talk with the white army. I told her I talked with a soldier when I first came to town. I told her of asking him of war between them and the tribes. He talked of the soldiers riding to the sub chiefs asking that they sign a promise of peace. I asked him if they declare war on the whites that live there; with no wish for harm to the army, is this legal??? He told me if they signed the treaty that it was illegal!! I then asked if he were sure that he had all the sub chiefs sign them?? He said I don't know!! She asked how an Indian could ask a soldier of this?? I told her I was white when I entered the fort!! She laughed and agreed.

I then asked the women of the tribe to name me as the "Sub Chief" to their tribe. I told them I would draft letters of war on the white rancher; and a letter to the fort of no wish for war with them. I told them we must turn this to a "Civil" action to keep the soldiers out of this. The woman told me of the last sub chief who tried something like this, and he was now dead. I asked her if he followed through with an attack on the rancher?? She said he was dead the day the paper was filed. I asked her to remain silent on this for now, that we would deliver the letters when the time is right. I told her we must train for war.

This was where my anger, My Love for the family; my very wits about me were out of my control. A lady from the tribe came to us and told us of White Feather being shot by the buffalo hunters. We all heard the thunder roll over the mountain.

I asked her to wait here for Mother Lozen, that it would be up to her. She got up and asked me to bring her to the reservation, that she will speak with the women of her tribe. I asked her if we must prove our "Bravery" when we come there?? She said we had proved it to the white and the red. She guaranteed our safety. I wished her Yah-Teh-Hey. I looked to the men who were looking back at me. I cut some branches from the cedar and said my prayers over us as I passed them to the fire. The white men then relaxed a bit as I did this. I was wishing for a victory over them as they burned.

When the stage arrived Mother was in a dress looking half white as they passed her the luggage. I saw them handing her a long wrap of the "Lances" as they unloaded the stage. Achak put them under his arm, and they started to walk my way. When mother was close, my eyes swung to the white man. They walked by with no notice of me. I waited till it was dark of the night before entering the fort. Mother was waiting near the man gate. After a hug of love she asked me if I understood what I had started?? I told her the bear and Coyote were talking to me!! She was in her buckskins now and I asked her of Achak? She told me of his corresponding with an Indian scout from the tribe. She talked of a warrior that he met at the tribel council with the tribe of the Coeur d Alenes. She talked of his dying wish for help. I felt the anger rising up in my Soul. I asked her if she would come with me for council with the women of the tribe of NezPierce, that they guaranteed our safety. She asked that I wait for her, that she needed to talk with Achak. I told her I would meet her at the back gate. A young girl from the tribe met me there and told me of three horses behind the fort ready to ride. I asked her to speak with Nalin and have her meet us at the horses. I told her of the code of five knocks to get her to the window. I asked her to have her slip out the window and meet with us. I then asked her of her horse?? She smiled and said she could only steal three!!! I told her we would ride double, that it's too dangerous to stay here now. She nodded and said she will meet us at the horses.

Mother came to me and handed me my Lance. We went to the back of the fort where an Indian soldier met with us and let us out the back. He talked of the warrior that gave his life for our help. He talked of being a scout for the soldiers and wished us "well" This is where the blood of yesterday caught up to me.

We heard the gunshots coming from town. We left the last horse and rode like the wind. Mother took two men down and I loaded Nalin. I took the third man to his death as Mother loaded the young girl. We went straight to the reservation. The young one lost her blood from a gunshot to her leg. She was barely able to talk when we arrived. Her mother took her down from the horse of my Mother, cursing the whites as she lifted her down. My mother told her she took the life of the white man whom had done this to her. She spit on the ground and thanked her for this. She told of the ranchers escape from jail!

Mother then said we had passed the point of no return. I then spit to the ground. She smiled and said lets talk to the women. We council with the women and we learned much of what they were facing. They talked of the rancher on Gold Hill that put the tribe under his foot, taking their land from them. Taking their cattle. And of taking their men. The women spoke of his army that he used to do this with. They said as one of the army of ranchers fell that two more replaced them. One woman told us of his "Greed"

Mother raised her hand to silence the talk. She spoke of eating a comb of "Honey" when the best is hidden in the bottom of the comb. She then picked up a honeycomb and looked at it. She spoke of the Queen be that lives in the hive. She said if the queen is dislodged from the hive that the bees come forth confused. She talked of the bees swarming ready to attack the first thing that moves. She talked of invading the bees at night when they're asleep and inactive. She said they would eventually rise in confusion to sting you!! She then smiled at them and said, "If your not fast enough."

Mother and I split the women in two groups. We asked what they had learned of the weapons of old. Some were comfortable with the bow and arrow and some with a knife. We each picked a young one to train with a lance.

Mother had planned the attack, and we trained them with this on our minds. We were watched during the day. We did our training them at night, as mother said it would be night when we do this. This went on for a month. The little girl from the fort passed away in the night. The women stood ready to give their lives for her spirit. Mother sent word of this to achak. She had me write the names of the family. She said she hopes to keep the fort busy investigating this. She was crying that she was only eleven years old. We rehearsed one last time with what we would do. Mother had given us alternate conceptions of the battle. She last said if any women is dropped that she must be left behind us. We had only enough to do this with no mistakes. We went silently to our lodging for sleep.

We feasted this morning to give us the strength we needed. And we lay down at noon for a rest. As the last soldier who watched over us left; we were painting our faces. Mother turned and smacked me across my face so hard that I nearly fell. I looked at her smiling. I turned and smacked my armour bearer with the same ferocity!!! When we were done with this I felt the Bear rise in our Souls. I gave the letter for the soldiers of the fort to the young boy to give to them when the morning arrived. The women at the ranch were instructed to deliver the declaration of war tied to an arrow to be stuck in the door of the ranch house. She said they would laugh at this. "Temporarily" We were ready for this; and we went. After we arrived mother gathered us near to her. She said she was waiting for the rain. The lightning struck. The thunder clapped. The rain started to fall. Mother said like I had; She had waited a lifetime for this moment in time.

Mother had sent two of the women ahead of us by a day to scout the grounds of the ranch and the men's movements. We were fourteen in number, and we were less then half of the ranch's army. The women counted thirty-six of them. The women were getting nervous and Mother calmed them. She said they just have more to be confused with. They had two guards out at night to protect the ranch house and cabin. They had two to protect bunkhouse. She nodded to me and I took the young lance bearer with me. As we split our duties I told her to imagine a Bear in front of her when she swings her lance. We had practiced the sounds of the night owl, which we used as a signal for ready. I gave the sound of the owl and our lances were stuck in their throats. We went to the bunkhouse and blocked the door at the front of it. I dowsed it with kerosene and my partner stood ready to light my arrow. I tied the handle to the doorjamb as tight as I could get it as my partner stood guard over me. She tapped on my shoulder and we saw a man moving our way. I pointed to the side of the building and she went there ready. She slit his throat and came back my way. We moved to our position half way between the bunkhouse and the ranch cabin. I stabbed my lance in the ground and had my fire arrow ready with my partner to light it. I gave the sound of the owl twice!!! As we saw them enter, my partner lit up my arrow, and I fired it straight to the door. The gunshots were sounding as two of the women joined me and we took station on the bunkhouse and we were dropping them as fast as we could.

---------------I saw Nalin fall. It was like it was in slow motion. With her eyes locked to mine as she fell. She had dove in front of a bullet meant for me. I still hear her screaming as she fell.-------------

I called out to the other two women to drag her to the horses, I tipped over the barrel of kerosene and ran to the house. I came through the door to my mothers back. And with our lances we settled the fight. Two of the women had the rancher tied up and were moving him to the door, and out of nowhere!!! The guns fired. They were shot dead. Mother took one as I took the other!!! When done, we drug the rancher to the horses. We threw him onto the back of one of them and lashed him to it, and Mother let go with a war scream as we waited. We had lost six of the women to the fight with the white men. Mothers steel gray eyes were blazing with fire as she looked to the battle. The bunkhouse was lighting where we were at, as mother was gathering the reins of the horse that the rancher sat on when a bullet hit her leg. I told her I have held them at bay for as long as is possible. I told her to ride. She turned her horse and charged the white man who was now missing his head. I took the life of three more men. We covered the remaining women's retreat as she came back with the last of the women, and we rode away.

I now felt the Great Spirit talk to me. He said---- "ENOUGH"----

We were all high on the mountain looking down on the reservation; as we dressed our wounds. The sky suddenly cleared. Mother had us leave her and two others there, and return to the reservation. She asked a vow of silence and told us to return to our lodging and wait to hear from Achak. We looked to the west and saw the fire burning. Mother said go now, the light is coming soon. We tied the horses near Mother; I prayed she not ride them. I checked her leg and told her the bullet went thru it. She just yelled at me to go. We quietly went to our lodges and rested from our battle. My heart went out to my mother, after healing from a battle before with her legs. I promised the Great Spirit I would fight no more. I asked for a blessing on Mother, that it was my hate in my heart that guided me. I will leave my lance on the hill and never again use it. I will fight no more. I heard a clap of thunder way off in the distance. "Like an answer to my prayers".

The next day the soldiers rode to our camp. They came to our lodging and forced us to kneel in front of them. With the soldiers to our backs holding rifles against us, they were asking who would speak for us. I saw the scout from the fort pleading with his eyes to do this. I felt murder in their heart, and stood up. He had the notice of war in his hand. The captain rode towards me and asked my name. I said the Lozen Xa'Xatas. He asked if I were responsible for the deaths of the ranchers?? The soldiers that searched our lodging now came before the captain and reported that no weapons were found in our lodging. He looked back to me. In English I said I count seven women that your soldiers have their guns to. I asked if this was as brave as he gets?? The soldier behind me knocked my feet out from under me, and the Captain yelled that's enough!!! He shouted to the back of them and had horses brought forward. We rode double back to the fort. We were placed in the stockade with no bread and no water. I forced a hole in the roof for our water. We took turns in the mornings to taste just a drop!!! This went on for a week. Two of the women were mothers of small children. I was asking for counsel with the Captain. He came to the front of the jail. I told the Captain of the children who need the suck of their mothers, that he would be as guilty of murder as any man who refuses this. He had two of his men take them to their children, and scowled at me as they locked the door. He asked if I were ready to talk. I told him I want the lawyer Achak to talk to before I say anything to him. He gave me the look of "Hate" and said he will see if the Colonel will allow this and glared to my face. I told him I have appeared in the courts of the white man, that I learned much of this!!! I told him I only want justice, I told him we will scream out a war chant day and night if he cant do this for me. I heard the women behind me start to chant. He said that's enough that he will see what he can do. We sat there for two days with no bread or water. I was about to give up when we were fed. A group of soldiers from fort Sherman rode in and took over the station of the guards. We were now treated much better; and they allowed us to use the men's shower. As I scrubbed the soot from my hair; and washed the dye from my face; I became a white Indian. The soldier assigned to me was in amazement as we walked back to the jail. Achak was waiting for me when we arrived. He held me close to himself and asked if I were doing well. I told him all is well that I have hidden my Mother, and I was praying she heal her wounds. He had a look on his face like I had just shot him. He told me he would hurry as much as he can. I asked of the soldiers from fort Sherman, that they treat us with respect. He spoke of how he had dealt with the issues for the tribe of the Coeur D Alenes and of demanding a provost marshal ride to fort Colville for a hearing. He asked me to not talk of my Mother yet, that he must keep his word holding with no lies being told. I said I took the vow of silence along with the other women that he shouldn't worry!! The guard said I'm sorry ma'am; I have to lock you up now. Achak hugged me and hurried to the to the court. We were fed beef and potatoes this night. We waited three days before we heard from Achak. The soldier let him join us for a council.

He first told us of the braves who took this to fort Sherman. He said they feared returning to the reservation. He told us of their attempts to speak with the white court of this, that their lands and belongings were taken from them. I told him we know of this, I apologized for not waiting for the courts to hear this. I told him of the men planning war on the rancher to get their land back. With so few men with no weapons it would have been suicide!! I told him of the families that had already given their lives for their land. I told him of the two men the rancher hired who were buffalo hunters that sat on the hill and used the tribe for target practice!!! That is why I sent them to fort Sherman; and that is why I kept their women close to me and trained them for war. I told him of sending the little daughter of Alona to his ranch with a notice of war for the land he had stolen, and of her return to our camp with both her legs broken. She had told us that the buffalo men had done this. She never delivered the notice. I explained my response to this, of how I went to the hill over the reservation and took the lives of the buffalo hunters with my lance, and sent their bodies back to them tied to their horses. I said this is "War" I was the sub chief who led them, and this was when you and mother showed up to help me. I told him I lost my sister Nalin in the battle with the rancher that took place there, and of holding the rancher with a promise to kill him if the white court; wont listen to our demands. He asked where he was held. I told him he's buried up to his neck in the sandy loam of the mountain. He asked if he were still alive??? I told him I instructed the women to keep him fed and alive. He nodded his head to me and went back to court.

The Captain was now in my face demanding I take him to the rancher. I looked at him and asked;" If the rancher could tell him, that which he doesn't already know"?? He said he needs his testimony for the court!!! I smiled, and asked him if his words hold more worth then mine?? He in a voice of "anger," said I would have my say in this!!! Still smiling I asked him who would listen to my words? The ones whom wrote the treaties?? Or, the ones whom are blind and don't enforce them?? He was ready to strike me with his fist. I kicked him between his legs and spit on him. The soldier behind me knocked me out with his rifel.

I spoke with Achak this night. I told him I feel trust in the soldiers from Fort Sherman. But I feel deceit from the soldiers from Colville. I told him if they want my cooperation they must allow me council with Fort Sherman. He asked if I could hold out long enough to see this? I asked the women with me if they would stand with me for this?? They all stood with pride.

He explained the military way of hearings to us and told of what can be said and not said about this. He named me the speaker for the women. He told of us of taking the scout with him to talk to the families, that were not many left to talk to. He told of them telling him of how they were hunted like dogs to settle the land issues. I turned and asked the women with me if they had the same history?? I turned back to Achak and told him to add five to his list. He called for the guard and wished us well.

After another week we were released from the jail. Achak asked that I show him my mother; With a quick wink of his eye!!! I refused to do this. The Captain and the colonel were both in my face. I repeated my demand for the Provost Marshall from Idaho to be part of this trial. A soldier struck me in my ribs with his rifle, and demanded I respect them!!! I spit at their feet!!! Achak now stepped in and held the rifel and told the soldier that he would eat it before he would let him strike me with it. I told him to let him strike me!! That he can show the court his bravery for this war when the court asks him of our injuries while being held as prisoners!!!

This night we could hear the soldiers from the fort Sherman arguing with our guards. They were passing insults to us. The women were crying as it went on. My side was so soar from being struck with the rifle that I could only sit up. I told them I would make them swallow their words. Leelaah came to me and asked if I were sure I was up to the punishment they give me. I called all of them to me. It made me smile as I looked to their eyes. I asked them all to stay with me till it's over. They all were crying as I held them.

After another week we heard our guards getting excited. I got up and held to the bars of our jail. The Captain and his soldiers was out side our jail cell telling them that I had won the battle. The Captain said the Provost Marshall from Idaho would be here next month. I was so happy to hear this I asked the guard from fort Sherman to release me, that I would take them to my mother!!! The Colville soldier smashed my fingers against the bars with stock of the rifle. The pain made me pass out. I awoke to one of the solders from Idaho holding ice on my hands. The girls were all around me. Leelaah was crying saying I will play the flute no more. I looked at my hand and this made me even more determined to win the battle.

The white doctor was allowed to see me next. He knew of my career with my music. He looked at my hand hanging crooked. He was upset with rage for the Captain whom he said, "allowed this to happen". He said he would sign a petition to have him removed with his company of men. As I looked at my hand; "It was worth it" I asked for a day to let the pain from this to stop. I made the women promise that I lead the soldiers to the camp of my Mother. The soldiers from Colville were slow to leave.

The next month I was released from the jail with a guard on me full time. I saw the Captains wife and children at the wagon as the four soldiers that were left to protect them were loading their belongings. I told my guard that they better be gone before we return from our trip to get my mother. He said he was not allowed to speak with them. I told him they would regret this!!

We rode to the top of the mountain and I had the guard fire five shots. After about a half hour they returned five shots to us. We rode to the camp. Mother had a splint on her leg and was walking. She held Achak in her arms. The women had the rancher tied to a tree. They had taught him to be quiet in the pit, and he was quiet as we stood there. The soldiers loaded him up and we rode. Mother Lozen told me that I make her proud to call me her daughter. That was all I waited to hear. She next looked at my hand; she said this looks recent!! She then said my music would suffer!! I told her I don't care if I ever play the flute again. She kept looking at it, and said "I Do" I could see her anger boiling over and there was nothing I could do.

Mother was taken to the forts doctor to look at her leg, and the rest of us were locked away. I was standing in the doorway waiting for her, and talking with our guard. The last of the Captains men were still loading a wagon making ready to go. I knew this was a mistake. Ken was walking with Mother with two soldiers to protect her. The men started making "Comments" to Mother Lozen! Oh man, was that the wrong thing to do!!! She knocked one to the ground and grabbed the hands of the other. She flipped him upside down and broke his fingers on both hands. It happened so fast that Ken was looking at her with his mouth open. Mother told me later that he said "Shame on you" She joined us that evening and discussed our defense. I asked her of the Fox. She told me she knows nothing of this, that she thinks she went to see her sister Ann. She reminded me of my oath of silence. She said she herself would die before the Fox saw the blood run. She spoke of "Chief Joseph", and of how he had to abandon members of his tribe to keep them moving towards Canada. She was left with group of them to protect them. She spoke of the army swooping in them taking the lives of all of them. She next looked to the air above her. She said the Great Spirit talked to her this night. She said he gave her the blood to lift her head, for she was mortally wounded in battle. She promised him to do what he said. Mother looked at me and said this was before you were "taken". I knelt in front of her and told her, this is where I was "Saved." She chuckled and said the court saw it differently. I asked if I would be able to speak with them about my feelings?? She told me I would have to "Craft" my words. I told her of crafting my words to speak with Ken!!! She was laughing now, and gave me the "one eye" look and said, #$%$%$#$ is not crafting!!!

Crafted or not, I was finally given time with Ken. After a long bear hug we sat down. He was looking me in my eyes, when he said, "You stepped in a bee hive" I chuckled and told him, "at least I'm sweet." He was just shaking his head. He told me of explaining to the military court of my situation. He said they wont listen to any testimony that uses some ones convictions, that its black and white! I told him I understand this, that it's not much different then dealing with mother. He asked if "Nalin" was part of my defense. I told him that she has guided me through all that has happened. I told him she was my first "Friend" other then you at this time, she looked at me as part of a family. With no questions; No judgments; She showed me her honest admiration of me. I told him she was my "Sister." He was shaking his head up and down, and said "Yes" that we will have to figure out a way to show the court the wrong that was placed on her. I told him it was placed on all the people in the tribe. He stood and told me that He and Achak will work on this. He asked of my mother sending me home away from the rancher Mister Richardson??? I told him I would have killed him where he stood!!! He said my Mother is wise!! He said I almost forgot!! Glen and his Father Atsa wrote a letter to the President. They asked to stand for you and your Mother. He said they should hear from Washington D.C. any day now. I asked him how they are doing???

He said they are as mad as a; three legged buffalo over this. I laughed as we said goodbye!!!

I sat next to my mother waiting. She asked me to leave it to the Great One. I told her I see the blood running from the battle with the Bear and the Coyote. I told her I hear the screams of the women that gave their life for us. She huffed out a laugh! She said they gave their life for "you" little one. I told her I thought I was dead when it happened, that I just kept fighting thinking I would fall to their bullets!! She said, "I know" She told me that she saw it in my eyes, as I commanded the women to move Nalin away from the battle. I started crying. I told her that I saw it in my dreams. Mother chuckled and said she had the dreams too! She said that when she made the last charge to save the women that she knew she would be wounded. I asked her if the Great Spirit led us through the battle?? She said you led it! The Spirit guided it. I had to laugh. I told her that she took down the "Bears" And I took down the "Coyote's. This made her laugh with me. She said you are right my Daughter; we now face the herd of buffalo that we watched grazing. I told her that's where my dreams ended, that we just stood there watching the herd move towards us. She laughed and said they were trying to trample us!!! She told me that she had the dreams much longer then I had: She asked me if I had ever noticed that most people Red or White couldn't look us in our eyes? I had to laugh; I said that's what I first saw in Nalin, that she was fixed to my eyes. I said that even Ken had his moments where he couldn't keep looking at me. I told her, she was like you mother; Nalin could read my eyes. She said she was my "Captain" in the battle. That she gave her life to save you. She said she was part of the herd that we watch over; with our "Eyes" he shows this to us. I asked her if the dreams would stop now?? She asked if I see the battle? Or do I see us watching the herd? I thought about this. I told her I still see the blood running, but I mostly just see us watching the herd, She smiled over me. She said this is where it ends. We next heard a voice in a whisper; Miss Lozen!! And the guard flipped her flute to her. She smiled like the sun. I fell asleep in her lap as she played the song of the river.

All the women in the cell came to us. Mother spoke to all of us now. She said to use our words wisely. She told the women not to speak like the crow. She said this only makes noise. She asked that we consider all words that we speak. To speak like the Fox! With pride in our speech. She said if we feel the Bear growling: to keep him quiet with a lance to his throat. She next spoke of speaking with the Coyote. She said he would make us stumble on our words. She asked whom would you rather speak with? The Spirit? Or the Coyote. She said her Spirit guide is the "Osprey" that he looks over the waters. She said he never dives to water without a hunger for the fish. She asked us to listen to our spirit guides. She said don't be one of the fish. We all felt her words of wisdom.

After six months of living on the jail floor it was our turn for trial. The land issues were settled first. The tribes land was returned to them after Achak took testimonies from the tribe and the whites. We were "All" behind him as he battled with his words to keep the boundary of the reservation "Untouchable" by anyone, Red or White. The rancher Mister Richardson was jailed for his part in the land theft; he was given five years of time to spend in a jail. The Ranchers men that remained were run out of town. They were told to never return. We were all of us happy now; it was nearly done.

I was next for my trial. Achak dreaded this most. Because I was the one whom declared war on the ranch, I was being held responsible for the deaths of the rancher's men. This was when I met my Aunt "Barbara" He didn't want to do this; but he brought up the fact that I was white. He had gone to the tribe of NezPierce and found the few people that were involved with this. After viewing the news reports; my name was, "Gloria Steen." My heart felt no reach for this name. I vowed to my Mother that I would remain Xa'xats to the last breath I would take!! My aunt Barbara stood with me as I announced this. The court asked her "Why?" She simply said; Lozen "was" her mother, She protected her with her life. The lawyer for the rancher then stood and said I had admitted my guilt!!! Achak countered with my being named as Sub Chief of the tribe. Barbara was crying now and stood and screamed at the court. She said "Shame on you" She asked Achak of the census. There were one hundred and sixty five names two years ago; and less then fifty today. She screamed that with alcohol, bullets, and sickness; that they had reduced their numbers. She asked if they were really this desperate that they claim the life of the few women that were left!!! I think she made her point!!! The lawyer then sat quietly. The judge then asked that we keep our testimony centered on me, that it was the fact that I led the tribe. Achak then held up a handful of papers with the names of the men that fell for the cause of this war. He only read the names of the women. He brought up the fact that I had "Declared" this war with the letter to the fort addressed to the Captain; and that I had given my surrender to him. He next held up the declaration of war delivered to the rancher. He told of the little girl who returned with her bones broken. He pointed to her sitting in a wheel chair; He said she sits in it for the rest of her life. He then said she walks taller then any man in this court!!

The court was now feeling our side of the issue. The local Sheriff spoke highly of me and told of how the battle started. I think he did more for the women then any man there. The judge then said anyone else. This was where Atsa and Glen stood for Mother and I. They were introduced as Father and Son. The judge shook his head and asked of this. Glen said it's a long story, and the court started laughing!! Glen turned to court and said there is no humor in this; He said these two women saved his life. He spoke of nearly dieing in the wagons that were stranded and the care that brought him back. He said they saved me twice when he survived from the wagon train. This was when they made sure I had a Father, He said his father gave up his job for the railroad, and sent me to take his place. He said laugh if you want too!! My father works for Mister Asher now. And I am the section master for the Burlington Northern. He said if you think this is funny!! I would lay down my life to repay them. He said he just couldn't believe the incompetence in this land. They gave me my life. And I Love them. You could hear a pin drop after this. The judge asked me to stand for my sentencing. Nearly everyone in the court stood with me as I stood to hear of life or death. The Colonel sat there looking at this!! He thanked everyone for standing with me. He then moved that I be sentenced with the women of the tribe; that I was the war chief that led them. He said that according to law I was no more guilty then any of the women that were charged with this crime. He brought up that I had legally declared war before attacking the ranch, with notice to the fort.

We all gave our testimony to the court. The attorney for mister Richardson tried to place the blame on my Mother for the attack on the ranch. He spent a week telling us lies. Mother now stood in her own defense and spoke to the court in English. She said she had formed a bond with the women of the tribe; that there were no men left. She said, "Yes" that she trained them to "Defend" themselves. She then pointed to mister Richardson and told of the battle and of saving his life. She said "Yes" I am guilty of training them. She said we had declared "War" on the injustice. She said we were out numbered. We had no guns. We had no men with the same strength of the rancher. We had nothing!!! She then looked to the Ranchers eyes. She said we had one thing they didn't have though. We had the Spirit of God in our hearts that gave us the advantage. We faced the battle with the Spirit on our side. She next spoke of the women who fell to the bullets. She then looked at Richardson. She said they gave their lives for that which is right. She said I lift not a weapon, that there is no need for that now. She said I lift the spirit of the women that you murdered, may they haunt you for the rest of your life!!

Achak next called the War Chief to the stand. He spoke to them of offering his surrender. Through his interpreter he told of the date that he did this. The court was becoming noisy. The Chief then held his hand up to the court, and it got quiet. The Chief said if they take the life of the Lozen and her daughter, that many more men would fall. He said; "if they wish to fight with a legend"!!! That she will trample you like the herds of buffalo!!! He asked that we "Stop" it right here. He looked at me and said; like the spirit of the little white "Tonka" that he feels we have proved our hearts.

The ladies and I were sentenced to one year in jail. The judge commuted our sentence for the time we had already served. He said the conditions of the jail were "intolerable." The judge shown Mother great honor; for raising me and for being my Mother. He recognized that we were at war with the white man, that we attacked them after the notice of the War Chiefs surrender. Some in the court were complaining of this. As the adjutant, banged his mallet on the table. He said his decision is "Final" With contempt he ordered them out of "His" court.

As we stood on the steps of the courthouse, I asked Ken to take me to Nalins grave. Everyone was looking to mother!! She nodded to him to take me, and Mother asked that I not stay there long. After arriving I asked Ken to stay with the buggy, that I wanted my time alone. He helped me down from the buggy and tended the horses as I walked the long walk to her side. I fell to my knees crying. I begged for her forgiveness for what I had done. I still saw the little girl who had given me the flowers. As I placed the flowers on her grave I told her that I miss the touch of her hand. I told her I valued her like she was the only sister I ever had. I told her, "I fought for you" my sister. I asked God why he hadn't taken me instead of you?? I told her I would do it again in a heart- beat!! I tried to play my flute over her grave. I couldn't do it. I looked at my crooked fingers. I promised that we would meet again!! -- "When the Spirit whispers my name"!! -- Aunt Barbara asked me to go.

It took a year of recovery from the battle with the rancher. It had changed so much in my life. I had recovered from loosing Nalin with the help of Barbara. She stood close to me through this time. She is my "Aunt" and I grew close to her as time moved along. She had no wish to return to Kentucky, She had lost her husband to the influenza. She had no children to bring her back, and kept her attention on me. She was about the same age as Mother Lozen. I had asked her not to speak of my parents and she respected this. She kept herself busy feeding the chickens and the horses. She was attached to all the animals and even fed the coyotes and deer that wandered threw the ranch. She bought scratch for the turkeys that would sometimes come by. Mother Lozen would laugh and call her "Cig'a'-mqal" which is NezPierce for "Animal" I told Mother of my pride in her. She said she's part of the herd we watch over. I chuckled and told her she was right!!

She mostly joined Mother and Bertha for coffee in town. She knew she could find me in the crafting room when she got home. She was standing in the door one day, and I realized she was wearing the same dress that she wears everyday!!! She had blond hair and blue eyes like mine' and was just not interested in beauty. She had given up on living a life after loosing her husband of twelve years. Fox and Amy stopped by just to see how we were doing. I spoke with her of this. I think I started a fire in her britches when she started thinking about this. I told her I would watch "Amy!!" if she would take her to town!!! I was thinking; "here we go" She grumbled and shook her finger at me. I ran to mother and told her I waylaid Amy!! And we planned a day with her for ourselves. I looked at her wall in her bedroom, and saw her lance chained to the wall with a paddle lock on it. I started laughing. She said that &(^%^$%#$^$% Ken and Achak did that. I silently praised God for their help!!!

Amy liked the trains. Amy's favorite thing to do was to have her Grandmother hold her on her shoulders and pull her arm up and down and get the engineers to honk the horn!!! This day they had a car full of sheep. The engineer had a man unload a little lamb for her to pet it. She fell in love with the lamb; and Grandmother paid for it. We finished the day with a rope around it walking like we owned a dog!!! What a spoiled little brat!!! We stopped at the general store and bought some feed for the lamb. The man at the store said to run her with the cattle and to build a feeder that only she can feed on. Grandmother had him draw a picture of the feeder and we returned home. She took the picture to Ken and had him do this immediately!!! He was laughing his butt off as he built it. With instructions from Amy he got it done. The next thing was to get her away from there so the lamb could eat!! We left that to Ken. It was getting late and Ken asked of the ladies and wondered where they were?? I told him of Fox taking Barbara to town for some shopping. He said that's why she was asking so many questions of the sheriff!! I hadn't thought about him till now, Ken said don't wait up for her!! I felt the Fox biting my aunts "butt". Mother just smiled.

When they returned home, aunt Barbara looked ten years younger. She was dressed in a nice dress and her hair was showing its gold, and she was beautiful. Barbara was busy scolding Fox for meeting with the Sheriff at the café for coffee; Fox couldn't fit a word in to her. I told Fox of the lamb that Grandmother bought for Amy!!! Amy was at the fence petting it. She gave me a look of disgust and said She felt Grandmothers claws in her!!! I said it was "her" idea and started to walk away. I could hear (&$%@#!! In the air, and I was laughing. I was watching as Barbara joined Amy with the lamb. They were talking, and Fox asked if she could take the lamb home with her?? I told her to ask her Mother of this!!! She said *&%&*$% You!!! I knew what she meant by that remark!! Barbara brought Amy back with her, and they named the lamb---"Nalin"---!!! I felt my heart fall from the top of a cliff.

I looked at Fox and threatened her with murder if she took the lamb!!! She smiled and loaded up Amy. Amy was screaming at her to let her stay the night, She told her Mom that---"Nalin-- would be lonely"---Tee-Hee. The Fox said %@$%$# and finally gave in to her, and Grandmother was smiling. She found a way to "waylay" her with no arguing. Ken told me I should be arrested!! I told him I would have Barbara ask the sheriff of this!!! Barbara said &*(^&%%. We were a normal family again.

Ann and Glenda were a team now. They were busy just searching for "Talent" They were assigned to California now where they had an office. Glenda assigned Ann to Spokane to search for talent here. I missed her so much I was ready to pull her from the window of the train!!! She stayed at the fox's house while she was here, but we were okay with this, because we had Amy here with us!!! Her Grandmother was busy spoiling her!! Because I would never do that!!! Tee Hee.

Things were rolling along now. The Fox would stop by to see her daughter. Amy and Barbara were having fun raising the lamb. Fox finally told her she must come home. Fox had to promise to bring her back soon though so her "Nalin" won't forget her!!! I said, I would see you tomorrow!! She said "*(^%$^" and away they went. Barbara was busy finding reasons that she needed to go to town for. She had bought two new dresses and just couldn't wait to wear them. The sheriff would take her for rides in the buggy, and stop to picnic along the way. She really was a lady, She told me of how she was raised. Sounded like a Fairy Tale to me. I had nothing to compare it to!! I asked for her help with Amy. When she looked at the Fox, she saw what I meant. She said she was "Rough around the edges." I agreed, like the boulders in the river, she was "Rough"

The Sheriff called her "Barb now, and she was fine with this. She was a beautiful lady and she kept up with this. She had found a new life to live with cheer in her heart. She loved the animals, the Sheriff, and Amy. Mother was fine with their relationship, but she still got after Fox about the way she lived. She told her she was "Demanding"

I wonder who she got that from??? Mother was after her now to have at least a second child!!! She made her feel bad when she spoke of my loosing Nalin. I asked mother to drop it!! And she got even worse. Fox finally gave in to her and said; I suppose you will steal this one too!! She smiled at her and said "ME" she said her aunt was guilty of doing this; that she just bought her a lamb. Oh WOW, I grabbed Ann and Ken and we went to town for dinner this night. Achak, Barb, and the sheriff joined us, and left Mom and Fox alone to argue. Mike finally showed up and thanked us for this. Barb brought Amy with her, and said forgive me God! With a look on her face like she had been 'stabbed', we were a typical family. We stayed late this night and just visited. Amy was tired and we eventually went home. Fox and Mother were looking at photographs of the family. It was like nothing had ever gone wrong. Barb, Amy, and Ann went to the barn to put Nalin up for the night. This was when Ann learned of the sheep's name. She came to me with tears in her eyes; She told me she was proud to call me her mother. She knew I couldn't sing. She Knew I couldn't play. She knew of the pain in my heart! I told her that Mother and I had hung up our lances now. She laughed about the one locked to the wall!! She asked of where mine had gone?? I told her I left it near Gold Mountain to rot away; that I could never do this again. She held me and said times are changing now, She spoke of the respect that people show her for the job that she does. She said she sees all the bright smiling faces. She said Glenda taught her not to let anyone quit trying that if you tell him or her; their no good, it's the worst thing you can do. She taught her tell them a little more work and to come back and see her. She smiled and told me it gives them "Hope" when she does this. I told her of Ken and I hoping she meets a man; that we both look forward to hearing little footsteps around our house. She sat up and smiled and said "Well" That she had met a man whom is in the motion picture industry, and he sets her heart on fire. She said it just happened so fast, that she just couldn't believe it. I told her it was that way for her Dad and I too, but to give it time with an eye on him. She giggled and said she has to be back soon, that Glenda will lift her hair if she's delayed!!! I said damn white Indians anyway. I thought I would need an ambulance she laughed so hard. She told me I still "Have it"..

Ken was heart broken when we put Ann on a train. He told her to come back with a "Bump in her belly" She said "DAD" and I whacked him. But I was laughing too!!! We headed for the café in town; where our friends welcomed us in. My hands were cold and I could barely hold a cup of coffee. The lady at the bar brought me a pair of dressy gloves, and helped me get them on. It felt like she had saved me!! She told me they were from France. I asked Ken to pay her for them; I really liked them. She just laughed and said she doesn't need them to work here! I said, you're new here; and asked her where she was from? She was laughing now and told of many towns that she was from. She spoke of her stop in Dodge City with a twinkle in her eyes. She told of a deputy that she dated there and of how he was shot dead. She was just smiling and said, "Those were the days"

I told her of my traveling around the country with the shows that we performed in. She said she remembers seeing me in Chicago when there were three of us in our routine. I told her that was long ago. She was holding my hand looking at it and asked of the trial that I went thru over that? I told her its like water under the bridge; that it's gone now. She laughed and told me she heard the tale of this in Butte Montana! She said the saloon was on the edge of their chairs as the trial went on and on and on! I started laughing and said yes it did!!! She asked me to write a book of what happened, that it was an interesting topic to follow. I showed her my hands and told her I have a sixth grade education. She kept looking at my hands, and asked if she could tell the story? I laughed and said you just told it to me! Ken said he didn't want a story told with the Red man being a villain in the story, that there are still people in this town that don't agree with the outcome of the trial. She laughed and told him of being run out of town in Montana for dating a half breed and having fun. Ken asked her if she would have a book published?? She was thinking now. She said if the publisher is good looking and likes to have fun she would do this!! Ken was now laughing and gave her permission to do this. She spoke of "Brepols" who published historical facts. She said there from Belgium and she has read many books that they published. She spoke of her education, which took my breath away. I asked her why she was working here? She said "Cuz its FUN" We were in stitches now. She introduced herself as "Bathsheba Goldberg" telling us that her family is Jewish. She said we could call her "Beth" I was fascinated with her name. I asked her to stop by our house, that I wanted to hear of her life. She giggled and said; "It's a deal"

I invited Bathsheba to dinner for Sunday night. She smiled and told me of eating "Kosher" I giggled and told her were having chicken!! She said, "That will work" I gave her a quick run down on my family, and she knew nearly every name. She had never heard of Fox, Ann, and Amy, and was looking forward to meeting them. I told her of Ann's new job in California and this peaked her interest. She spoke of moving pictures, that it's all the "Rage"

As we sat down for dinner Bathsheba asked to say Grace. She did this with a spirit of glee in her voice, and asked a blessing on all of us. Amy demanded she sit next to Bathsheba, and we did the switcho-chango. She hung onto every word she spoke. After we were done with dinner we went to the front of the house. Bathsheba took Amy to the big chair and had her sit on her lap. She took a Bible from her bag and read her the story of "King David and Bathsheba". I was totally engrossed in the story myself. She would read a verse and stop and explain it, and let Amy ask questions. She would then cover it quickly and move on to the next verse. This went on so long that Amy was asleep in her arms. My whole family was there with us as Bathsheba placed a blessing on her and passed her to Fox; She said; "Goodnight my little Angel, I pray you stay in Gods keep" We all felt the power of her Prayer.

Mother asked me the next day what the difference was between the "Great Spirit" and Bathsheba' s "God" was. I told her I don't really know this. I told her of asking her the same question. She told me that we all see him differently. She said if you ask anybody this question it's different. She told me that she saw you guide the family with your Spirit. She said feels her God talking to you as you speak. Mother next asked of the book that she carry? I told her it's called a "Bible"!!! I told her of Ann using and of how it taught me of God!!! She asked if she used it to speak with the Spirit? I told her I wasn't sure. I said she told me of the curtain that hangs between Heaven and us. That; he pulls it back to speak to us. She picked up her flute and started to play it. She stopped. She said she was; "Very Wise"

It was a short time later when we had our own personnel Rabbi living at Fox's house. It made Barb cry, but I sent Nalin the sheep up there too. I told her to "get over it"!! Bathsheba started taking Amy with her to the Synagogue; they would stop just to say hi to the Rabbi. I couldn't believe it, but Fox never complained of being robbed of her daughter. I asked mother of this. I told her she smoothes out the roughness of the Fox!!! She said she makes everybody feel the Great Spirit when she speaks; and that's all she ever said of this. My family was "very" happy again. Life had slowed down to a stage of comfort. The people in town had forgotten my problems in Colville now, and it was just a legend.

"MY" daughter Ann was married in Paris France. She was so happy with her job, her husband, and her life she now lives. Kenasher was still grumbling about no bump in her belly, I whacked him and told him to grow up. We didn't have much anymore since the Colville incident; But we still had each other.

Amy had her Bat-Mitzvah when she turned twelve years old. Bathsheba was so proud. It was the first time I had ever seen my mother cry. The Rabbi asked mother say grace over her in Sahaptian at the close of the ceremony, and everyone was so happy.

Bathsheba had married the younger Rabbi and was as free with her spirit as always. With Amy in tow, she would travel the town, never looking at anybody as being anything but a person. This is what Mother saw in her too!!! We both knew we weren't capable of this and we left this up to Bathsheba. Ann would stop in when she could. The three of them would load up Amy and do the town. Fox, Ann. And Bathsheba. They were a generation that never faced war. They taught Amy a new way to live!!!

Mother spoke to me this night of being the Family Elder. She spoke of times that were hard for her to make a decision. She spoke of the Fox and how she was raised. She admitted that she wasn't perfect!!! This made us both laugh! She next spoke of the Sacred sevens she was born under. She said the Spirit talked to of this. She told me it's more then her love of her daughter that brings this to her mind. She spoke of protecting her from the blood. She said there was no way to do this for me. She depended on me for her protection. She asked for only "my decision" to name Fox as the family "Elder" I thanked her for her decision. I told her she was wise; I felt that Fox wore her wisdom with fairness to all of us. I told her the hate in my heart has never gone away. I asked her to be named this before she leaves to talk with the Great Spirit that looks over us. We both chuckled!!! She Asked me what she would give her to present this to her. I instantly told her; your "Lance" Mother made Achak unlock it- tee-hee and she polished it till it shined like a star. She made me promise to help Fox with this. I told her I would on one condition!!! She looked at me with suspicion!!! I told to just tell her; you "Love her" This brought a "rare" smile to her face!!!

Mother gave me her usual "what's all the fuss about?" But Ken and I set up the backyard for the occasion. I made Ann come home. Glenda came with her. With the whole family, music and entertainment was not a problem. All of our close friends came for this too. Mother was in a state of disbelief over all this "fussing" She said this just isn't done this way by the tribes. I told her it's special to us!! Ken just chuckled and told her she saved his butt more then once. He asked her to just enjoy this. She finally said.-- "I will" We just had a ball with this. Amy made Grandmother wear her buckskins. She tied the sacred feathers into her hair. She still shone with beauty and pride. Ken attached new Eagle feathers to the mast of her Lance. Mother gave them a blessing when he was done. Fox and I set up the tubs for fry bread and beef and Fox made Mother sit and watch us. Mother said %$#@$%%%$ just trying to help!!! Fox just told her to play her flute with the song of the "Coyote" Mother stuck her toung out at her and begin to play!!! I told her thanks Fox!!! She gave me her "Evil smile" That's my sister!!!

Achak had his friends from the tribes bring their drums for the ceremony. It was hard to imagine how much time had passed. Most everyone including Mother spoke in English now. It made me miss the days of the old ways. When Barbara and the Sheriff arrived they brought her famous apple pies with them. We blended together like glue. Mother told me there is no ceremony to this. She said the Chief usually walks by you and tells you; "You are an Elder"!!! I told her to fake it!!! She shrugged her shoulders and said "ok" We had more fun that day then we had in a long time. Fox won the bandana pick up race with Ann. They were both still attached to their horses. Fox kept Ann's horse at her house, just incase she wants to race!!

For the passing of the staff from Mother to Fox, Mother rode Ann's horse to her and handed her the staff. They both leaned into each other and hugged as the people were applauding; Mother told her, she-- "Loves her"-- It was Mothers idea! It made Barbara cry. Damn woman had me crying too. It was "Beautiful" We took pride in our "Heritage" even if it was invented by us!!! Mother just wished to keep it alive. She lived a "Tuff" life! With very few words, she kept us on our paths. She never asked us to do anything that she wouldn't do herself. She stopped us from doing wrong. Sometimes with just a "look" From her steel gray eyes that contained "Fire" "Lozen" translated, means "Woman Warrior" She was all that and more!!! She had a soft side, that not many seen!!! This involved "children" Early on: it was cuddling up with her on a cold winter night. Later on it was like my sister Nalin. It was like someone drove a stake in her heart. She knew that it killed me to loose her. The women from the tribe told me of her loosing her soul when Nalin died. She sat on the edge of the cliff for three days not eating or drinking anything. She played her flute non-stop day and night. This was her way of crying!!

When Mother Lozen passed away, she asked for the youngest and the oldest. Achak led us to her room and kissed her goodbye. We both sat on her bed and Amy was crying. Mother took her hand and commanded her to stop this. She spoke of her childhood and smiled as she told us; of the rivers; of the camps; and the wind. She said she could never have imagined having a family so large that it fills her soul like the stars in the sky. We promised her to listen to the Fox. She squeezed hard on our hands; as she passed her Soul to our Creator. As her hands relaxed she was gone. She is a Great Spirit that lives in our Souls now. I took Amy from the room still crying. Bathsheba held her and brought her to earth "with her smile". I went to ken, and held him. We all stood there in silence. That's what "Mother liked best"!! The drums stopped. We all said a silent prayer.

She was buried near Colville at the reservation; and Achak went back to the East. My family now named me the Grand Mother of the family, and I wear this with pride. I give Mother Lozen the respect she deserves. I give Fox the "Family Trust". Mother was buried next to Nalin. This was her last wish. She gave us the courage, the Love, and the respect that we carry with us. I wish I could give it to the world.

I gave Mothers flute to Ann, and asked her to play it. This she did, before leaving her grave. She played the tune of the Bear and the Coyote, and I recited the words in Sahaptian, for that was a time long ago!! I asked her to keep the flute. I asked that she keep mother Lozen's spirit with it. I asked that she bless it before lifting it to her lips. She had always shown "Honor" for her Grandmother, and I trusted her with this. She put her arm around me as we walked away. She turned to her grave and said "N'de Varlebena" which is "Love forever" to her Grandmother, and the wagon was rolling away.

She was part of the west!! She lived in times of turmoil. When I shut my eyes, I still see her slim body clad in leather holding her lance. I see her fighting the Bear; I see her playing her flute. I feel her; "Quiet Love",---- every day.

THE LOZEN

Annie

My Grandmother Annie told me the story of Lozen. She grew up in the eighteen hundreds. Annie described the "Lozen" as a lonely Soul. My Grandmother was a friend of all that she met. The color of their skin never made a difference to Annie: she was a student of the tribe of the NezPierce to learn of healing from them. She was "Very Spiritual"; she was a Bible believing woman. She spoke a bit of the Sahaptian Language, which she had learned in her travels. She described the Lozen as a "beautiful woman". She spoke of her eyes that were "wolf like" She said they looked at you with "fire"!!! Annie said she used them to read your Soul. She spoke of her connection to her family. She said she was "Stingy" with them. This made me laugh. She told me of her guiding her family with her flute that she played endlessly. She spoke of feeling relaxed as she listen to her play it. She smiled, and said; "She made it "Talk to the earth." If you listen you will hear it. With her eyes shining; she took me there!!!

She mostly talked to her daughter "Xa'Xats to hear the story of their life. She first told me of their scars. She was near crying as she told of their mussel-toned bodies; that were torn from their way of life. Annie was "Disgusted" with their use of swear words. She would rise up and curse their use of the words!!! While laughing at her, I can just see her finger waving in their face. She said unlike Lozen that Xa'Xats had many friends. She said she was mostly quiet, till she got mad!!

She told me of how the family would kneel in front of the Lozen. She said they did this if they wanted to talk. She made me feel the power of the Lozen as she spoke of this. She told me of the family council. It seems that anything that involves the family, must have the blessing of the "Family Elder." She spoke of her "Wisdom" in the matters of her family. She said that she would sometimes take days to make a decision. She said her decisions were final, that there were never arguments over that!!!

I hope I have given the feeling of Lozen's "Authority" in my story. My Grandmother made me feel it. Whenever she would tell me a tale; it was always with a message of; Love and Hate; Right and wrong. Trust and mistrust. She was quite a "Lady" I miss her!!! In Fact; I miss her more.-----every day!!!

Robert C Wright

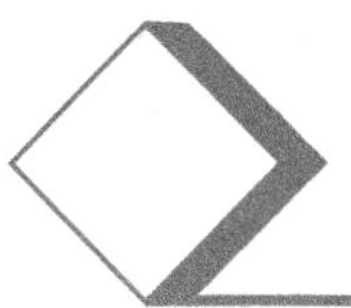

About the Author

Bob Wright

I was born in Spokane Washington in 1949 and soon after my Father took job on the coast in the little town of Houghton Washington. This is where my memories begin. I remember all the men there telling their stories of action in W.W. 2 and Korea. Times were just starting to change in the world.

We lived in what was lovingly called the "Projects" there in Houghten which consisted of old military barracks that were shoved together and stuffed full of old vets that were really old to me, they were in their late twenties most of them; and at that time in my life they were "OLD".

I am now in my 70's myself and it makes me laugh to think about it. But I still recall the stories and the way of life was much simpler then, as it was before cell phones and computers, and if you didn't have a church key you couldn't drink a beer or a pop.

My Mother and Father were as Loving to me as any parent could possibly be, and bought a house near Totem Lake; which was called "Mud Lake" at that time, and that was where I was raised. I had two brothers and I was the youngest of them; and I could tell you stories that would make you laugh and cry of those times.

My Father was educated in the wilderness up near North Port here in Washington State. My Grandfather had a homestead there and when my Father had finished the sixth grade he was taken out of school to work on the homestead. My father took me there and showed me the old cabin they lived in as he grew. He had 11 brothers and sisters who he shared the cabin with. An outhouse, and a lantern for they're lighting and stories that were full of hard work, honesty, and Love. This is why my Father was insisting we get an education. His education he told me was "robbed" from him and I had better listen to him or he would "Lower the boom on me"

So I took the word of my father and attended school in Juanita in an old wooden schoolhouse that still stood there at this time and began my journey of life. I enjoyed History and Math, and science, and all the classes that I took. Except for one. The class that I had no use for was "English". Do I regret this now?

My father became angry with me, as my report card would arrive showing that I was a straight "D" student in English. I did just enough to pass the class and would not listen to my father. I remember him telling me of a story of when he was young and the Sheriff had "CON-FIST-TA-CATED" his rifel from him as he carried it into town. I thought to myself, hey, it's just a "word" !!! And didn't try to correct him. I would then show him my grades in math, history and Science with a look of pride on my face!! He would then snarl and growl at me and tell me I would live to regret this. Man, was he ever right about that. As I struggled to write this story I think I saw him Laughing at me and shaking his finger at me saying, "I told you so"!! My Mother would protect me and say "he will do better next time", Mothers aren't right all the time; but bless you Mom as you saved me from a pants warming party!!!

Life moved me on as Uncle Sam moved me to the Air Force. The Vietnam debacle was raging and there wasn't time to even think about what I wanted to do with my life as I marched off to war. Those were times of struggle and times of fun during that experience. This is where at the age of eighteen I wound up getting married. That was DUMB, but I had two kids now and there was no turning back. So when I got out of the service I took a job running heavy equipment that my Father had taught me to do from the time I could see over the steering wheel of the Michigan loader that he operated. I started my career here in Spokane where I sit as I speak. I Love my kids with my whole Heart and I have had several different wives on this journey and I give each of them a blessing for putting up with me and for their help raising the kids.

It was spring in the year of 2009 as I was retuning from the winter that I spent in Phoenix. I was in a hurry to get home and had been having trouble with "TIA's which is a minor stroke and just kept on driving. I pulled into Provo Utah and got a room for the night and was still recovering from a TIA that I had the night before this. This is where the story started. As I awoke the next morning my head was "fuzzy" and I went to the shower. I remember the firemen scooping me up from the floor with the shower rod and curtain wrapped around me, and my right side was gone. My mind was gone also, and I don't remember much about the ambulance ride or anything after that.

The hospital in Provo couldn't help me so they loaded my bones and shipped me to Salt Lake. This is where they were about to pronounce me as "DEAD" but for one doctor that said "ahh,,,, Ill give it another try". He blasted me with the old Tesla coils and I started to breath again.

As I looked around the room I didn't recognize any one and I felt like a Garbage truck had just run over me. I fell back to sleep as the drugs they were filling me with; they did this for "me". The next time I awoke I saw my family was with me and they asked me if I recognized them. I said; "YES". The doctor was amazed by this and told me of dying from the stroke and of how he couldn't believe I could speak.

My family was tired after this whole thing went on, and left me to get some sleep for them. My head was spinning and I was starting to have memories of dying that made no sense to me at this time. From deep in my sole I heard a voice tell me to get up and walk. So I rang for a nurse and of coarse no one showed up. I heard it again, "get up and walk".

After unhooking the drip line and pulling the cables from myself I made a few trips around my bed with my arms on the bed as I traveled. This is where the lovely large lady came into my room and started chewing on me like a bear feeds on fish. She was busy yelling at me as she hooked everything back up to me with the bedside manner of a bear. I got back into bed and said "Sorry" With her joyful spirit she got me all settled and this is when the doctor arrived to see what the fuss was about. I told him, I was asked to walk. He asked by whom?? I told him "I don't know"!! He just shook his head and said "can you walk" I told him if his little darling will let me " yes I can walk " With a laugh he said well I gotta see this and told the darling to un hook me. With a look that would stop a freight train on her face she did this for me, and I got up and did three trips around the hallways there in the hospital. The doctor just shook his head and said let him walk.

After three days of walking I was ready to run around the halls and I checked myself out of the hospital. With the doctors telling me don't do that yet and the lovely young large nurse just a smiling, I climbed into my Sons truck and was traveling again. I was Dumb. As we went out of Salt Lake I was going over in my head what I had seen when I was dead. I wasn't sure if I had dreamed this or if it had happened. I told my son a short version of what I had seen. I then asked him if I was NUTTS. After some consideration on this he turned to me and said " Well: you never lied to me before Dad". This was the point where my life started to change. I remember fighting with the voices of the small soul to keep them at bay as they went on day after day.

I built a little horse ranch in Pasco at this time, and lived with a sexy little gal that I eventually married, I was Dumb. The voices in my head continued and I struggled with them, as they were never tired of it. I think they thought it was fun!! I tried to tell my then wife of the voices and I had changed my life to look at things with the Love of God for that which I viewed. I felt my Grandmother moving me.

My lovely young bride then smiled at me and with a soft loving smile, she told me....."I WAS NUTTS".....She then ran off with a dashing young cowboy and lived happily ever after. Or at least for now it's that way. Tee Hee. So I returned to Spokane where I was born and was still struggling with the voices. I have to admit it was driving me crazy and I had no explanation for this. This is when I asked of God,,, "Why am I here" He made feel that this is where I belong!!! I don't know why?? But I felt it.

This is where Ayiana appeared to me. She was like, a thought? Like a ghost? Like a; Spirit. She didn't haunt me, but I felt her presence. Though I have never spoken to her with words; we have bonded together with the glue of our souls. She started by showing me way off in the distance a little girl standing there holding a kitten in her arms. She looked like a little Indian girl who was playing with her cat. This kind of scared me at first!! The first couple months she just showed me her "kitten" I learned to use my sole to ask her what this meant?? She spoke to me with her emotions and I understood this was important to her as she held the kitten, and even held it out to me a few times. It was like talking to the wind as we bonded our souls together with some rough trails in the beginning. Now when I'm lonely and tired I think of her and the Love fills my soul for her and all she has taught me to live this life. I eventually figured out that she was showing me her name was Ayiana after she had nearly shook the cat to death, I went to the internet and looked up the meaning of a small cat in Apache and there it was, Ayiana. I felt her smile. I looked for her name in Apache because of a recent history with the tribe. The youngest brother of the family that worked for me popped into my mind. His name was "Albert Teechee" He had told me many stories. He spoke of "Spirituality" that exists in his tribe. He told me of speaking with an Elder of his tribe. He told me he was 103 years old when he died. He talked of war with the "Hopi" He told him of there spiritual ways. He spoke of their "God" named "Yahweh" which is close to the name used by the Jewish people!!! He next spoke of a preacher named Arnold Murray. He told of him reading the Bat stones. I checked. He was right. Turns out the Jews discovered America!!! He was convinced they were descendants of the lost tribes of Israel. This made me laugh. I checked on this and he was right!!! I thought; WOW. What's next?? He had lost his mother in-law and said he speaks to her all the time!!! He told me she was his "Favorite Spirit" That she guides his life down the trail they choose. I thought he was "Nutts" But Hey!!! Who Knows? I sure don't!! I returned to Phoenix and talked to him. I asked him when he sees her, is she far away??? He thought for a bit. He said no, sometimes she's near him!! Sometimes she's far away. I told him I only saw Ayiana once up close! And talked of her eyes. He got the "Shivers" as he told me of a lady when he was young, seems she went by the name of "Wolf Eyes" I went to my truck and brought back my notebook and showed him the close up I drew of Ayiana!! He put his hand on the picture and looked up to the sky. He said he felt the "Love" flow between us" He said it would be there till I die!!! I chuckled and told him I'm not ready for that!! He asked if I had a choice?? I laughed and told him I feel Gods strength each morning, as I open my eyes to this world. His little brother "Sam" now joined in with us. He said we give him the "Creeps" He told of us of a phone call he got from his long dead aunt. I started to get the creeps!!! So I don't know!! I ask if I dreamed it?? Or did I see the doors and the light?? This happened years ago now. When it's mentioned I'm proud to tell the story of this. There are no words to describe the light and the voice; or the feelings that I bring up from my heart. I call it the Backdoor to Heaven. It was surly not the pearly gates. I felt the spirit of others who walked right threw me. I wasn't scared when it happened. I describe it as being like a brief wisp of wind. I'm sure I asked him many questions!! Like why does the walkway only go to the left!! It was a "black obis" to the right. If God or the Great Spirit walked through it, it would be on his left side. Why are the doors made of wood?? And what creates the light??? What happened to my body?? As I looked I could see no legs. It felt like I was walking and talking!! "But; how"? I don't know. I have read everything on near death experiences!! There is nothing close to mine. Did I dream it?? Or did I see it? So I don't know what to say!!! You tell me!!! It has changed my life for the better. I now deal with the Indian "Ghost" "Spirit" or "Angel" I don't know!! I keep her close. I feel her love when I need it! She's there. She stands beside my Grandmother "Annie" as strong as strong as the steel in a bridge!!!

Ayiana then showed me the tail of two souls that her Mother had taught to her when she was young. She showed me not to listen to the voices of the small souls that they were like a picture taken in time, and they make no sense. She then showed me that it was my big Soul that was at the doors of judgment as my small sole remained on earth. I came to understand that which she had shown me as time moved us on.

She then showed me myself, and the way that I have lived. Like a buffalo that runs wild through the prairie. Work was first and my family was second. I apologize for this to my kids and my wives. She next started showing me "Books" After a struggle; I now understood that she wanted me to write this book! I told her NO, that she was asking the wrong guy. She smiled at me.

She then showed me myself at the funeral of, I don't know; a relative of hers? I'm not sure. He was a half brother to one of my wives; I had only met him once. He was a "Nutt" but a good one, and I enjoyed meeting him as we talked of Vietnam and how he had gotten into drugs while he was there. Soon after this he died from an overdose!!! I went to his funeral. I don't know what got into me but after the Chief had given his views of him and told of the good things in his life; we filed by his grave to toss a handful of earth onto his casket. As I looked down to his casket I kissed the earth that I held in my hand and said a prayer to God for him as I did this. I still feel her smiling as she showed this to me. It was the first time I saw her face clearly. She appeared to be fifty or sixty years old. She was "actually,---attractive"--- I drew her picture but I did her no justice!!! Especially with her eyes!!! Man; they sparkled like the light of the Sun.

As time went on it was like having your guts pulled from your stomach, as she demanded I pay attention to her. I did my best to ignore her but she was insisting that she was right. I couldn't take no more of this and finally told her "OK"; and like a typical woman she had won this fight and showed me lets begin!!!

The first thing I had to do was learn the language of the Soul. When I had died and went to what I call the backdoor to heaven I never seen anybody, never traveled through a tunnel, I Never saw the pearly gates. But I remember the Voice of a spirit that spoke to me, with Love and understanding, and when he laughed it gave me Love, freedom, and courage to come back to earth to finish my life. I had seen it with my spirit as I looked at the two big doors in front of me, with the light pouring over them like; water? I guess, and I felt the warmth of the light with Love as it flowed over my spirit. I was told I cannot look beyond those doors or I will never go back. I understood. And I returned to earth in the blink of an eye.

As I sit here now I "think "you fool you should have dove head first through those doors", you dummy!! and wonder why I didn't! But after dealing with Ayiana; I try to understand now why I was led back here. We took the task of writing this book to our hearts and worked on it daily as we started. She would show me an adventure in her life and I would draw pictures of that which she showed me, and I was slowly getting the picture in my mind to write this book. She showed me that she "Gives me the Words" for this book and I showed her the medicine I take for heartburn as she shows me her life at the age of about five and the next thing I see she's fifty something. She showed me she was sorry for this but time doesn't work there in her happy hunting grounds the way the clock ticks here for me

I call this; "walking in her Soul". She explains her life to me with emotions that she felt as her life was lived. If she felt it,, I felt it. It was not easy to deal with her losses and it was like the backdoor to Heaven!!! When she held her head high with pride in herself. I just Love her to death. She reminds me of a love I once had for an Indian girl in Idaho long ago and this was Betty. She was as sweet as an apple that hangs from the tree. I still see her face giggling with the high cheekbones and her beauty was inside and out. She lives in my heart. I ask the Great One to look after her.

I would describe life as a "Dimension" That we live in; with a "Curtain" that exists between Earth and Heaven. I thank "God" for lifting the curtain for me when I talk to Ayiana. I just know it works when I see and feel her. It's the answers to; how I do this; I don't have.

So this is the history behind this book. I hope it makes you laugh, and cry, and you feel the emotions that we felt to write this. We all deal with our problems, on our own mostly; it doesn't matter if its drugs, death, or any problem you face in your life, as it was for Ayiana. Its Love that matters and Love that conquers all the grief that we feel as we live here. For I can tell you that when you get to the other side that all the things here on earth that were such a problem for us are "GONE". And as you look back to earth you will understand and "feel" what I'm telling you now.

For as my life began here in Spokane. I now enjoy the sun and the wind on my face as I stand here; and feel the grip of Spokane in my blood. It took a lifetime to learn this. That it's not the Gold in your pockets. It's not the strength in our pride!! It's the "Love" that we take with us. It's the love we shared along the way. And I wish Love for all who walk the face of this earth for it's Love that gave me the answers I have found.------------

Maybe!!! Love is all we need to know!!!

Robert C Wright